The Other Side of the Fairy House

A Christmas Time Travel

June Foster

Kelly Cordova

Acknowledgements

Thanks to my sweet granddaughter, Caroline Cordova, for her assistance in writing the rock-climbing scenes and for her knowledge of the sport.

Thanks to my patient co-author, Kelly Cordova, for her research and for plotting such an amazing story.

Chapter One

Late November

Fifteen feet above the ground, Madison clung to the vertical sandstone rock. Her weight centered over bent legs. What was her next move?

Below a stand of pine trees grew on either side of the boulder. The rumbling of the river, as loud as a train, made its way to her. She shivered with the cool breeze but remembered. Rocks were more tacky and easier to climb in cold weather.

She braved a glance down at some of the guys watching from below, arms extended to catch her if she slipped. Beside them, Melody, her best friend, clapped her hands. "You've got this."

Blowing a long strand of hair out of her face and with her right foot firmly in a pocket foothold, Madison pushed down and straightened her leg, propelling up. With a smooth deliberate move, she hooked her left heel round the narrow overhang. She grasped the bulging rock and pulled her body up, stomach resting on the cold stone.

Black boots met her gaze. She followed green

trousers up long legs to a black belted waist, broad shoulders and into the glare of a park ranger.

The man stared down at her. "Ma'am, this area is closed to climbers. Let me see the permit you received when you registered."

Madison pulled herself to the top of the rock and fished into her side pocket. She held up the form she'd printed off.

A wisp of recognition floated to her brain. Then she remembered a skinny, shy guy from high school. But this couldn't be him, towering over her, despite her five-foot-eight stature.

The guy glanced down at the group below. "I need to talk to all of you."

Madison's heart pounded as she followed him down a short scramble on the back side of the rock. Their whole group had registered. So, what was the problem?

At the bottom, Melody, along with the others, stared, eyes open wide. "What's going on?" Melody said.

The forest ranger peered at Madison. "You're on t—t—t … " his voice trailed off into the repeated sound as her eyes met his, "Tennessee State Park land, and you need to properly register to climb here."

"We did register," Melody grasped her hands onto her waist, "before we climbed last week."

The ranger squinted like the sun blinded him, and he glared. "You're required to register online every time you climb. If you had registered, you'd know that this area is closed for Peregrine observation."

"What in the world is that?" Madison muttered.

"You-you might not take this seriously, but the nesting behaviors of the raptors are important to this area." The expression on the ranger's face softened. Was he thinking of cutting them some slack? He rolled his brown eyes as he glanced at the sky. "You know what, I'm not going to fine you. But if you want to climb at the park again, you'll need to take the orientation class."

Heat rushed to Madison's face until her cheeks burned. "We already did that," she took a breath, "online."

"Well, you're going to have to do it again. You obviously weren't paying attention. And this time, you will attend in person. Now, I'll need your names and phone numbers."

As each of Madison's friends filed by, the ranger jotted down names and numbers in his notebook. After the last hiker spoke, the ranger slammed the book shut and walked in the opposite direction. Then he stopped and turned around. "Oh, I'll g—give you fifteen minutes to pack up your gear and clear out of the area." He sauntered away, his wide shoulders swaying with his long strides.

Melody gave a low whistle as he strode away. "That guy's hot."

"If you say so." Madison tapped her forehead and stared after the park official. "Seems familiar."

"Who?" Melody giggled.

"He reminds me of a skinny, dorky little kid I knew from high school. He also stuttered when he talked."

"Hmm, well this guy is cute."

Madison clenched her jaw. Who was this park ranger?

Ben marched away, his heart pounding in his ears. *She didn't recognize me.* Madison Montgomery from high school—the girl he'd had a crush on. Seemed like ages ago. If he could forget those days, he'd be happy. The way he made fun of her red hair and called her carrottop. He'd never let on the real reason he said those things to her, that he liked her.

Ben had to admit he'd changed. He chuckled under his breath. His grandma called him a late bloomer. Short and thin in high school, but when he hit his growth spurt in college, he'd grown like a weed.

Near the rangers' office, his colleague Andy walked toward him. "All clear on the section north of the river."

Ben picked up his pace to catch up with his fellow forest ranger.

"Yea, nothing but the cardinals trilling in the trees. How's everything with you?" Andy turned as Ben caught up.

Ben shook his head. "I found a group of climbers in the Peregrine nesting area. Can you believe it?" He blew out a breath. "They're clearing out now."

"Did you stick it to them?" Andy snickered.

"Sort of. I told them they needed to come in for orientation before they can climb again." His chest tightened. "I can't believe some people won't follow the rules."

"No respect for our bird population either." Andy repositioned his ranger hat as he stepped around an azalea bush.

Ben fist bumped Andy's shoulder. "You'll never guess who one of them was. Remember Maddie Montgomery?" Ben searched his friend's face to get his reaction.

"You mean the yearbook photographer who was so stuck up?"

"Yea, that's the one." Ben slowed as they approached the building a hundred yards ahead.

Andy grinned. "So, is she still drop-dead gorgeous?"

"Yes." Ben's face heated. "I doubt she was impressed. I got all tongue tied when I recognized her." Ben shook his head trying to make the memory go away. "But she didn't remember me."

"No worries, buddy. She isn't worth stressing over."

Ben walked side by side with Andy as they neared the rangers' building. People could change. He had, right? Maybe she wasn't as high-and-mighty as she used to be.

Ben held the door and allowed Andy to enter first. They had plenty of paperwork to fill out today.

Ben sat at his desk in his office with only a small book shelf and two chairs and basked in the afternoon rays slicing through the cedar tree out the window. The waning light cast a warm glow on the short cliffs across from the headquarters competing with the lights on his miniature Christmas tree sitting on his desk. Working for the state of Tennessee was great, but someday he wanted to spend his time as a US Forestry Agent. Instead of sitting here filling out papers, he'd spend time designing and implementing beautiful landscape structures. He tapped his pen a few times on the wooden desktop. Someday.

Chapter Two

Madison gripped the steering wheel as she guided her ten-year-old Toyota around the curves and bends in the recently cleared road. The Donaldson State Park maintenance crew kept the road drivable in the winter months, for which she was grateful. She tightened her jaws as she glanced at her friend Melody in the passenger seat. "This is so stupid—making us come to the ranger station to take a silly class. They're just punishing us for being avid rock climbers." She grumbled. "Not everybody would get out in this freezing weather to scale the mountain walls."

Melody drew her animal-patterned parka with the fur-lined hood closer around her. "True, but look at the positive side. Maybe we'll see that cute ranger again. So what if he stutters a little."

A picture of the skinny boy in high school that shied away from everybody bounced into her mind. "No, thanks. But I hope to learn more about our beautiful state park."

Madison slowed as she spotted the sign that indicated the ranger station lay ahead. She turned left off the main road and followed the now familiar paved route to the facility.

Melody pulled her hood over her light brown hair and chuckled. "The others in our group are going to be sorry they didn't come here with us today when they want to climb next weekend."

Pulling into the station's parking lot, Madison laughed. "Well, they'll have to get up early on a Saturday like we did and attend another time." She cut the motor and opened the car door to get out.

Madison's heavy boots crunched on the gravel the forest service had laid along the path to the front door of the log building. She shivered with the brisk wind that blew past her. She opened the door, Melody following.

Inside, a blazing fire burned, sending warmth and a smoky aroma through the room. Behind a wooden desk which boasted a park service plaque, an older ranger smiled. "Good morning, ladies. How can I help you?"

Madison glanced around. If she had her vote, they'd hold the class in front of the fireplace. "We're here for the park orientation." She stared at the man with a kind face. "Actually, we're here in protest. The standoffish ranger who threatened us said we couldn't rock climb anymore until we took the class. It's ridiculous because we know this area."

The man behind the desk lifted his index finger. "I'm sorry, ma'am, but we have our regulations. The ranger was only following rules."

"Well, I still don't think he made a wise decision." Madison's pulse beat faster than the continuous shooting mode on her camera. "He's not very realistic with his—"

Melody tapped Madison's shoulder and cleared her throat.

"Care to voice your complaint to me, Maddie?"

Maddie? She spun around to face the source of the deep voice standing to her left and gasped.

A tall guy who could give a male model competition glanced down his straight nose at her.

Madison eyed his name tag. Ben Taylor. Was this the Ben from high school? She'd never have believed Ben Taylor would grow up to be such a good-looking guy.

"Ben? How are you?"

"Maddie Montgomery. It's been a long time. I figured you didn't know who I was last weekend when you were rock climbing in the Peregrine area."

Heat shot across her cheeks. "Er, yes. Seems we made a simple mistake. Everyone does, right?"

"Everyone who doesn't read the regulations."

She swallowed the remark she wanted to make. He was merely an old grouch. "You remember Melody? She's also one of the offenders."

"Hey." Ben nodded at her and offered a grin. "Where are your other friends?"

"Who knows?" Face still hot, Madison threw up her hands and glanced at Melody. "Well, we're here, aren't we?" She hiked her fingers to her forehead in a salute. "Following the rules."

"Excuse me." Ben turned to speak to the middle-aged man behind the desk.

Melody whispered in Madison's ear. "Hey, lay off the sarcasm. You've given him enough of a hard time."

Madison smiled at her. "We'll see." The Ben Taylor from high school was nothing like this young man. And to think, he was the same one who issued them the warning and the notice about the class.

Ben turned from the main desk to her again. "So, Maddie, what are you doing these days?"

"Maddie, huh? I haven't answered to that name since my senior year in high school. I'm working at Cliffside Realty Group as a photographer."

He ran a hand over the light covering of brown whiskers on his chin. "I do some freelance photography myself."

Maddison liked the ring of her old name, Maddie. "You were always so studious in high school." And shy. "No doubt you went to college."

"Yep." Ben straightened his muscled shoulders and lifted his chin. Evergreen State. I g—g—got a degree in landscape architecture." He studied his feet.

Though still unsure of himself, he was the same guy. But this Ben had grown several inches and probably spent his free time lifting weights. She had to admit that he looked great, and he wasn't wearing a wedding ring either. Was he attached to someone?

"You two are the only class participants today. Follow me, and we'll get started." Ben headed toward the west side of the building and a door leading to their destination.

Madison followed his long stride toward their classroom. Memories from high school filtered into her brain. She had often snubbed him, and on occasion she didn't speak when he said hello. She shoved the memories to the back of her mind. Time to focus on the orientation.

Ben clicked off the slideshow presentation and glanced at the two women. "So, you can understand why we go to such great efforts to protect the natural habitats of our bird populations. The Peregrines only came off the endangered species list in 1999, and we don't want them returning to that classification."

Melody raised her index finger. "I'm amazed at how fast the Falcon can fly."

"That's right. They can reach speeds up to two hundred forty miles per hour." Ben smiled at the attractive woman with hair piled on top of her head with some kind of a clip.

Why had he avoided focusing on Maddie? Maddie Montgomery who made his heart race? And why did he stutter again? He forced himself to make eye contact with the gorgeous woman, red curls cascading down her back and shoulders. Her eyes the color of periwinkles growing outside the ranger station in the summer. "Do either of you have any questions?"

"Yes, what other activities are available in the park this time of year besides rock climbing?" Maddie asked.

Why did she have to look at him that way? To show white teeth in a wide grin? Making him remember how in high school he'd been attracted to her. "Want to see a frozen waterfall? The hike to Prism Falls takes about five hours there and back. Steep in places but worth it."

Maddie crossed one leg over the other. "Why do they call it Prism Falls?"

He released a slow breath. She seemed interested in his talk. "Good question. In the summer, the sunshine creates prisms shining through the mist. But now, the falls are frozen."

"So, you recommend Prism Falls?" Melody said.

"There are a couple of others that are easier to get to, but Prism Falls is the most spectacular."

Maddie smiled. "That sounds like fun."

"I need to remind you, though. Watch out for falling icicles on cliff edges."

Melody clapped her hands. "Sounds like an adventure we can't skip." She jumped up. "Excuse me. I want to buy some postcards out front."

Despite the chilly day, sweat covered Ben's forehead and underarms. He hated to see Melody leave. She was a buffer—someone to shield him from Maddie's full attention. The high school Maddie had always made him nervous because he wasn't Mr. Popular. But then, they were no longer in high school.

Maddie rose from her chair and brushed one of the bouncy curls from her cheek. "Do you remember Jack Parsons?"

If Ben was still a kid, he'd want to disappear into the woodwork. The guy was only the hero of their school. "Yeah. The quarterback on our football team. He—he was Mr. Popularity."

She chuckled. "Well, not any more. He's in a Nashville jail for tax fraud."

Ben took a step back. He'd always wanted to be like Jack—well liked, handsome, sure of himself. Strange how that worked out.

She gazed around the room and back to him. "What was your favorite memory from high school?"

The worst question she could've asked. Thinking about those days was like remembering a root canal. "I—I suppose joining the photography club. We got to go on some cool assignments for the school newspaper." And Maddie probably didn't remember him from the photo walks when they shot pictures of different locations to gain each other's perspective.

"Hmm." She squinted, as if trying to remember. "I suppose my favorite memories are being on the yearbook staff. I enjoyed going to the football games, too."

Football. He'd wanted to try out but was too skinny to make the team. This journey down memory lane didn't help. He was an adult now, so his past relationship with Maddie didn't need to bother him anymore. He ran a hand through his hair and started toward the door to the lobby. "All right, M—Maddie. I hope you learned something from today's presentation and will take it to heart."

She stared at him as if summing up the morning. "Thank you. I did learn a lot. I'm sure Melody did, as well."

The two women walked out of the lobby into the snowy day. Ben needed to avoid Maddie Montgomery in the future. Being with her brought back too many painful memories of the dork he was in the past. And his boyhood problem with stuttering always seemed to return in her presence.

Andy strolled toward him. "From the look on your face, the orientation didn't go well. What happened?"

Ben shook his head. "No, that went okay."

"Then why the long face?" Andy persisted.

Ben scraped his boot on the hardwood floor. He didn't feel like talking about it.

Andy slapped his shoulder. "You're attracted to her, and she's not interested?"

"Okay, okay." Ben glared at his friend. "In high

school the kids she hung with mocked my stuttering. I wanted to get to know her better, but if she wasn't with them, she was ignoring me. I might as well have been invisible." Talking about his school days was as bad as trekking in the forest and coming home with his ankles eaten by chigger bites. Annoying and painful.

Ben returned to the conference room to put away his supplies. No need to fret about Maddie as the odds of seeing her again were remote.

Chapter Three

The next Friday, Madison stopped her car in the lot across the street from the trailhead leading to a popular rock-climbing area. She turned to Melody in the passenger seat. "I wish we could get another ranger besides Ben to lead the group."

"Why don't you want Ben to go with us?" Melody zipped up her heavy parka.

Madison shook her head and opened the driver's door. "Oh, never mind. I suppose he makes me uncomfortable." She glanced around at the few climbers who had arrived. "I made a reservation for ten this morning. It's nine fifty-five now." She blew out her breath in a long stream of smoke that looked like a misty cloud. Surely, the park ranger would be along any moment.

Melody slipped on her heavy gloves and walked around to Madison's side of the car. "Didn't Ricky and Sarah promise to come along today? I wonder where they are."

Madison pulled her wool cap over her ears. "I saw one of the guys at the grocery store yesterday. He said they scheduled the orientation for earlier this morning and would show up with the ranger." She opened her trunk and reached in for her gear.

Melody pointed down the road the way they'd come. "I see the ranger's vehicle."

The ranger in a white Ford Explorer with the park emblem on the side pulled up, followed by a red four-wheeled drive truck.

"Hey, Madison, I think we have a different guy than the one who conducted our orientation." Melody pulled her gear out of the trunk.

Madison sagged against the side of her car. Thankfully she wouldn't have to contend with Ben today. She wanted to enjoy the climb instead of worrying about what he thought of her.

The rest of their group piled out of the truck and followed the ranger toward them. Nope, the blond guy definitely wasn't Ben.

The ranger waved, a wide grin on his face. "Morning. I'm Andy, your climbing guide."

A couple of guys returned his greeting, and then busied themselves getting their supplies together.

Madison laid her crash pad on the ground and set her climbing shoes, snacks and water on the pad. Then she folded the ends like a book and hooked the clasps together. She slipped the crash pad over her shoulders like a long backpack, clipping a belt around her waist for support.

After she finished getting her gear ready, she joined Melody standing next to Andy. "The rest of the climbers are pokey." She glanced at her watch. The day was wasting away.

Finally, the group of ten circled around Andy. He pointed across the parking lot. "Okay, let's go. Follow me up the trail."

After a short hike, Andy stopped in the middle of the rocky path. "Blue Mountain has extensive routes for traditional climbing and rappelling, but we're heading to one of the bouldering areas. As you know, we won't use ropes and harnesses on the low overhanging rock."

"Sounds good." One of the guys at the back of the line fist bumped another.

"In the past, hikers have left behind trash." Andy grinned at the girls. "That's one reason I get to hang out with you today."

Ricky caught up with Andy. "We're a careful bunch of climbers. No worries."

With an easy smile, Andy nodded. "Awesome."

Madison smirked at Ricky's words. Sure, they were careful with their trash, but she'd seen Ricky leave a couple of soda cans behind in the past. She kept a brisk pace on the flat, rocky path.

Andy turned to the group following him from behind. "It's a great day for climbing. Cold but dry." He slowed as the rocks loomed ahead. A boulder fifteen feet high came into view. "This rock will be an easy problem."

"What? I don't get it." One of the new guys spoke up.

Madison grinned as she remembered her first climb. "It's like using code. *Problem* is a word a climber uses for a route on which they'll climb. And if you *send* it, that means you made it to the top without falling on your first try."

"Oh, that's encouraging." The new guy laughed and set his backpack against a tree. "Honestly, I'm a little nervous."

Madison patted his back. "You'll do great. Besides,

this first problem looks easy." A cluster of small bushes made a good place to stash her bag while she squeezed her foot into her climbing shoes. First to chalk up, Madison approached the boulder.

Two guys arranged the pads at the base of the rock.

"Let's do it." One of the most experienced guys shoved them together. His ebony eyes shining, he signaled Madison he was ready to spot her.

Madison took a deep breath and reached for the first crevice only big enough for her finger tips.

"Yea, Madison. You can do it." Her crew hollered.

The encouragement boosted her confidence, and she anchored her toe in one of the small holes and then shifted to another fingerhold above her. Glancing down, she smiled at the pair of hands extended, ready to catch her if necessary. Thankfully, no ranger with green pants standing above her watched this time.

After a successful climb, Madison clambered down the back of the rock.

Melody gave her a high-five. "Good job."

Pulling on her jacket, Madison's stomach rumbled. She reached into the snack bag and grasped a package of sliced apples. The feeling of exhilaration after a successful climb always made the strenuous effort of scaling the granite worth it.

After an hour, the last of the crew made the short climb.

"Who's ready to move on?" Andy signaled with his hand above his head. "Next stop, Watchman's Roof."

On the trail, Madison lagged behind to walk beside Melody at the back of the line. "You doing okay?"

"You bet. If I could, I'd spend all my weekends like this out in the fresh air. Do you ever look at one of the boulders and wonder what kind of people camped near that rock a hundred years ago?"

"Funny you say that. Some of the caves around here have ancient drawings on the walls. Ever since college when I took world history, events of former years fascinate me. My dream is to publish a book featuring my photos of the area and include restored vintage photos of past inhabitants."

"I'm usually stuck in an office behind a computer every day so I admire your career."

The trail narrowed so the group marched single file, crash pads on their backs like a row of dominos.

"Careful of this crevice," Andy said. "You've got to jump."

After the split in the path, Andy turned to the crowd. "This is Watchman's Roof."

An enormous rock that resembled a shallow cave with its overhang appeared ahead on the right. Madison set her equipment on the ground a few feet from the base of the rock.

Melody's voice wobbled. "I still can't get used to the possibility of falling. This rock looks like a challenge."

"Not to worry." Madison patted Melody's shoulder. "With our large group, we'll have more surface area covered with pads to cushion a fall."

The new guy on the team stretched his triceps. "Yeah, but I hope I won't need one."

Madison took a swig of water, adjusted her shoes, and rubbed chalk on her hands.

When Ricky began the climb, he reminded her of a spider as he crept along the ceiling. Could she do the same out here on this rock?

Madison took a deep breath and began her climb. After only a few minutes, her muscles ached, and she had to grip with all her strength to keep from flying off. A few moves later, she reached her hand out. Her foot lost traction, and the move jerked her to the ground.

Andy rushed toward her. "Hey, you all right?"

Madison massaged her forearms and frowned. "Yeah, but I'm disappointed in myself for not making it." She gritted her teeth. "Next time." Madison pulled out her camera, the latest Nikon model. "The next best thing to climbing is taking pictures of people climbing." She zoomed in on Melody's grip on the rock. "So, do you climb with Ben?"

"Sometimes. He's pretty good. Not as good as me." Andy raised his brows and chuckled. "You know, you don't seem mean."

Madison fumbled her camera missing the shot. "What are you talking about?"

"Ben said in high school you were hard to get along with. I think he used the word mean. You don't seem that way to me."

Madison held her breath until her chest burned. Mean? Yea, Ben had approached her and asked about the photography club. Her friends had called him History, and she had laughed. No doubt, it took him a while to figure it out. History repeats itself, like someone who stutters. "I used to tease him some, but he always bugged me about my red hair."

Madison focused and captured Melody in a perfect shot. If Madison could go back in time, she'd redo her petty high school behavior. She glanced at Andy. "Well, maybe if Ben hadn't been such a know-it-all ... " Her cheeks burned red. "And a smart aleck." Had the cold wind heated her face, or something else?

The miniature fairy lights on Ben's table-sized Christmas tree twinkled, sending sparks of color around his office. The decorative lights reminded him of every spring and summer when the park was home to thousands of fireflies, giving the appearance of fairies lighting up the mountains.

On his bulletin board, a couple of handmade cards asking him to his niece and nephew's annual Christmas program at their church hung with thumbtacks. He smiled. His brother's kids loved sending invitations to Uncle Ben each December. He'd better write down the date of their program. Didn't want to forget and disappoint them. And he wouldn't dwell on the thought that his brother went to Maddie's church and her mother directed the program.

Christmas.

Ben's favorite time of year reminded him of the birth of his Savior.

Laughter and the chatter of male and female voices emerged from the front lobby. Either another tour group had arrived or Maddie and her friends had returned from their rock-climbing expedition.

A tap landed on the door, and Andy sauntered in, his nose and cheeks red. "Can't complain about your friend Maddie's group today. They cooperated and followed instructions."

"Must've been extra cold out there. You look like Rudolph the Red Nosed Reindeer." Ben enjoyed the sound of his own howl.

Andy slipped off his gloves and warmed his hands at the space heater in Ben's office. "Take note for the next time you're overseeing the group. They kept their body temps up with all that strenuous climbing. I had the privilege of standing around, making sure no one trampled over our protected plants and fungi and almost froze."

"Good to know. Did Maddie complain about not getting to climb in the restricted area like she did that last time when I confronted the group?"

In front of the heater, Andy turned his hands to the other side a moment and then rubbed them together. "Not really. She was pleasant and easy to get along with. And she's a good climber. She outdid a couple of the guys."

"I suppose you're right about that. She's an avid fan of the out of doors."

Andy turned from the heater to face Ben. "I probably have to give you an apology. I got her riled up. I told her how you thought she was mean in high school."

"What?"

"You know. What you told me about last week after your orientation."

Ben folded his arms over his chest. "She rubs me the wrong way, but you didn't have to tell her that."

"Could be she feels the same about you." Andy relaxed into the extra office chair.

Rubbing his brow, Ben rose from his chair and stood in front of Andy. "What are you talking about now?"

Andy cleared his throat. "She, er, she said you were

a know-it-all."

Heat flamed Ben's face, and he resisted the urge to jerk Andy up by his jacket and yell in his face. Instead, he tightened his fists.

"I'm sorry, Ben." Andy stared at his feet. "I see now I opened my mouth when I shouldn't have. It's just that— "

"Just what?" Ben took a deep breath. Once again, he had to calm his irritation.

"It's just that she was really nice. My comments merely slipped out." Andy stood, threw up his hands, and headed toward the door. "I'm staying out of this from now on."

Ben followed him out of the room. He needed a break outside in the fresh air. Hoping to avoid the group, he grabbed his heavy parka, scarf, and gloves and headed out the back door into the chilly afternoon. The cold air bit his nose and cheeks, but he expected the change. "How about you keep your trap shut next time?"

"Righto buddy. We're good?" Andy turned around to high five Ben, but Ben lowered his hand at the last second making Andy stumble over his own feet.

Ben tramped off toward the stand of evergreens on the eastern side of the building. What would he say the next time he saw Maddie? He rounded the corner of the building.

Someone in a heavy jacket and head down careened toward him. A couple of red curly strands of hair peeked from her cap as her head snapped up.

His heart raced.

Maddie blinked flakes of snow from her eyelashes.

So much for avoiding her. "Hey, Maddie. How was

your climb?" Maybe he could talk to her now, to make peace.

She glanced up. "Oh, hi, Ben. We had a great time. Some of the guys were new to the sport, but they're really picking it up. Andy, he's a good guide. I'm so glad we got our climb in before this freezing weather blew in." Madison shivered and pulled her hood over her cap.

He placed his hand on her elbow. "Listen, Maddie. I know we had our differences in high school, but do you suppose we could put it all behind us?" He wasn't sure he could let it go, but he would try.

Maddie faced him, shoulders square. "Don't know if that's possible. Maybe I'm just too mean." She lifted her chin and walked toward the parking lot. She strode to her car without looking his way.

Ben scratched his head. *That didn't go well.* More than ever, he needed to avoid that implacable woman.

Chapter Four

Madison stopped on the steep path to catch her breath. "Yes." Her kind of weekend—bouldering one day, hiking the next. Though her muscles ached, the upward trek to Prism Falls was worth the effort, in her opinion. The others trailed behind, the curving narrow pathway hiding them from view. Thick evergreen bushes poked their branches onto the path as if telling her not to get too close to the edge.

Melody caught up with her and smiled. "Hey, you're not giving up?" Her light brown eyes twinkled with mischief.

"Are you kidding? We've hiked this far with less than an hour left. I can't miss this beautiful, immovable cascade. But can you explain how Ben and Andy happened to both come along on our adventure?"

"I thought it a good idea to have a couple of professional guides since our entire group is supposed to come today," Melody grinned. "I may have mentioned to Andy that they should accompany us. Next time, don't rush off from the climb so fast."

Madison shrugged and headed up the path again.

"Hey, you're not really mad, are you?" Melody called from behind.

"I don't know. I don't want to see Ben again." Telling everybody she was mean. "What kind of forest ranger is he? Walking in the back and leaving us girls to lead the way. I could do with one weekend where I don't run into him. Is that too much to ask?"

"You really have it out for him, don't you?" Melody panted as she picked up her pace.

Around the next bend, a huge boulder blocked the path. Good. An opportunity to change the subject. "No telling when that rock fell onto the path. Look at the covering of moss on the sides."

"Yeah, but how do we get around it?" Melody scratched her forehead.

"We could climb over it, but I didn't bring my climbing shoes. Let's get through on the right side. Looks like we have a little room." Madison turned sideways and edged through, clearing the rock to the path on the other side.

After a few yards, the narrow path opened into a wide meadow. No doubt, in spring the area would be covered in wildflowers. Now, piles of melting snow were scattered over the ground. "How about a break while we wait for the others?"

"Right." Melody said. "Too bad a couple of the guys had to work. They would've loved this trail. At least Ricky and his little sister Sarah could come." She lowered onto a flat rock and pulled out her pink water flask.

Andy and one of the other guys trekked into the clearing.

"Where's the rest of the group?" Madison wanted to keep going but hiking protocol said they shouldn't leave others behind.

Andy guffawed. "You know Ben. He had to point out every plant along the way."

Was Andy as annoyed as Madison?

The sound of rustling in the evergreen bushes off to the right caught Madison's attention. Then a snap like a limb breaking followed by the shuffling of leaves. An animal? Some of the others in the group? "Did you hear that?" Madison glanced at Melody.

Melody took a swig of water. "Hear what?"

Madison shrugged. Hopefully a wild animal wasn't following them.

Sarah arrived, walking along beside Ben as they approached the group. "So, in the spring we reinforce the path with mulch." Ben looked up. "You guys ready to go on toward the clearing?"

"You bet." Andy adjusted his backpack.

Madison and the rest of the group followed Andy, trekking up the trail toward the open area. She glanced behind at the stragglers.

Near the back, Sarah tapped Ben's shoulder. "Awe, look at that." She leaped off toward the thick bushes.

"Wait!" Ben called.

Sarah dropped to all fours and crawled toward a group of dense bushes. "There's something caught in there." She either disregarded his warning, or she didn't hear him.

A juvenile black bear poked its nose out from a small hole underneath an evergreen limb.

"How cute." She stretched out her hand toward the small animal, probably wanting to pet it. "He's all alone."

Madison pushed through the group at the edge of the clearing and gawked at Sarah.

"Don't touch the cub," Ben ordered.

Farther into the forest, leaves crunched. A deep rumble and the vibrating ground warned them, a bear approached.

Terror raced down Madison's spine. If Sarah didn't get away from the cub, the mother bear would charge her.

Sarah grasped her throat as she looked toward the growling bear who appeared out of the thicket.

Ben lowered his voice. "Back up. Slowly. Toward us." He eased an aerosol can of bear spray from his belt.

Sarah stepped behind Ben, her hands shaking.

"The rest of you," Ben hissed. "get—get in back of me."

The group slowly moved behind Ben.

Madison's eyes widened.

The mama bear rose up to her full height.

Sarah screamed. "Ben."

The cub's mother growled and advanced toward Ben.

"Everyone. Yell. Make lots of noise. Now." Ben sprayed a cloud of the mist toward the angry creature.

Unable to budge, Madison's legs seemed frozen to the ground. As if moving in slow motion, she forced her limbs to step behind Ben along with the others.

The bear flinched, shaking her nose from side to side, and produced loud snorts.

Andy pointed up the trail. "Back up slowly. Let's get out of here."

Behind Ben, Madison inched up the trail with the rest of the hikers. She sneaked a peek behind. So far, the bear hadn't followed.

Andy caught up with Ben as they walked farther in the direction of the waterfall. "I think we're safe now. Phew. That was close. And on the positive side, you all get an *I Survived a Bear Encounter* t-shirt."

Melody traipsed toward Madison. "Sarah should've known better. I can't believe Ben didn't give her the wilderness 101 speech to never mess with a bear cub."

"Well, she knows now." Madison breathed harder as she trudged up the steep incline until the terrain leveled off.

To the side of the path, the ground dropped into a valley below. The mountain ranges rose one in front of the other like backdrops on a stage, each a different shade of gray and blue. Madison pulled out her Nikon and snapped a shot of the snowy peaks.

Melody moved closer to the drop-off. "That should make a good one."

"If only I'd had my camera out for that bear incident." Madison tightened her jaw.

"Don't worry. It happened so fast," Melody said.

"Hey, how you doing?" Ben beckoned to them.

Melody bounced from one foot to the other. "Nerves a bit shattered, but I can't wait to see Prism Falls."

"You're going to love the view." Ben said. "It's beautiful in the summer, but in the winter—spectacular. Trust me. The falls … well, I'll let you see for yourself. This way."

Along with Melody, Madison followed Ben up the trail to the right. The path curved and then straightened through a canopy of Fraser fir and white pine. The ever-present stream ran parallel to the path. It dipped and cracked through the middle of a frozen river bed.

Madison's heart rate increased. The falls couldn't be far now.

A rustling sound followed by twigs breaking and crunching sounded farther into the forest.

A chill raced down Madison's back. Was the mother bear following them? She tugged Ben's backpack. "Did you hear that?"

"Don't worry. I doubt the mother bear would follow us. And smaller creatures run when they hear someone coming."

Madison took quicker strides to keep up with Ben's lengthy ones. "I love the out-of-doors, but I don't care to encounter another bear."

Ben chuckled and pointed to the path ahead.

A doe and a fawn crossed the road. The doe's white tail blended into the snow-covered forest as mother and baby scampered away. "There's your beast."

Relief flooded Madison. Having Ben here brought safety. "That was pretty heroic what you did back there when Sarah encountered the mother bear."

"Part of my training and what I do. N—n—next time, I recommend that all of you carry bear spray." He stepped over an exposed root. "And avoid petting wild animals."

Madison had to admit that. Ben knew his job.

A few minutes later, Ben trekked around another rock in their path. "Are—are you ready for this?"

Madison gasped as she stared at an exquisite ice sculpture frozen in place. Gray rocks framed the work of art with white tipped pines as a backdrop. As if time had stopped, the water paused in midair.

Ben grinned. "This spot is known for proposals of m—m—marriage. I saw a guy on bended knee holding a ring out to a girl. I think she said yes because he stood, grinned, and pl—pl—placed the ring on her finger."

"Awe, that's so romantic." Maybe she'd get a proposal like that someday. She secured her camera, ready for the spectacular shot. Today's hike to Prism Falls proved to be better than she could have imagined. The fog rolling through the hills, sun sparkling like diamonds on the half-frozen river, bare branches arching to the sky, she never expected the winter to display such beauty. And the biggest surprise was Ben. In high school, she hadn't given much thought about him except as someone the gang teased and called a loser. But today he had shown competence and courage in the face of a vicious bear. Had she misjudged him? What else would she learn about him?

Ben snapped his mouth shut. Why had he told Maddie about the proposal? Sure, in his silly teenage fantasies, he'd dreamed of proposing to her, especially after he saw her vulnerability.

The kids she hung with weren't up to her caliber. They never were, but she seemed embarrassed of her blue-collar roots, from the comfortable home she lived in with her thoughtful parents to the fact that her mom and dad cared about being a part of her life. If she could've seen what he saw—the lostness of those other kids whose parents worked to give them everything they wanted and nothing that they needed.

He'd come across her one day when they'd been especially cruel to her. She tried hard to hide her tears, but they still fell down her cheeks. He'd sat by the riverbank with her not saying much but listening to her sniffle.

"Why are you being nice to me?" she'd demanded. "I've never been nice to you."

He'd smirked. "You've been mean, actually." He nudged her with his shoulder.

"So, why?" she whispered, her lips trembling.

He'd shrugged. "Maybe because I know you're better than that." It had been hard, but he'd forced himself to stand, to move away. "And if you ever need a real friend, I'd like to be that for you."

What about his cursed tendency to stammer? He didn't remember stammering that day, but he was sure he had.

And now, she'd brought it to him again. His youthful speech impediment had returned. But why? For years he'd worked to control the habit. But around Maddie, no matter how hard he tried to speak with fluency, the words didn't always flow. He sounded like an idiot. *Lord, free me of this tendency.*

A warm, gloved hand rested on his arm. "Ben, are you okay? You look like you're in another world. I saw a path behind the falls. Wanta go?" Maddie nudged him farther behind the waterfall.

Ben's ranger persona returned, and he tugged her

away. "It's not a good idea. I d—d—don't want a chunk of ice falling on our heads." The urge to protect Maddie washed over him—unlike the bear incident when he only did his duty. Though she was strong and athletic, Maddie's feminine nature showed through today.

As much as the desire overwhelmed him, he needed to face reality. Maddie turned him into a blubbering idiot, and his chances with her were zero. He had to get his mind off that impossible woman.

Later as he drove through town heading home, the Christmas lights spoke of the upcoming holiday. Decorated trees outside every store, wreaths adorning the light poles, lighted Christmas villages in store windows. Thinking about how they celebrated Jesus' arrival into the world gave him perspective. Including tomorrow night's Christmas program at his brother's church. Besides, he had to keep his promise to see his niece and nephew perform.

Ben pulled into his apartment's parking lot and climbed the stairs to his second-floor residence. Between now and tomorrow evening, he had to forget that Maddie went to his brother's church and that her mother directed this year's Christmas pageant.

Chapter Five

Ben scooted into his brother's car in the front of his apartment. "Thanks, bro, for picking me up this evening."

Dave nodded and put his Chevy in gear. "No problem. Your place is right on the way."

"Uncle Ben, Uncle Ben." His nephew and niece called from the backseat.

He swung around to his six-year-old niece wearing wobbly pink ears and a wooly suit. His eight-year-old nephew was dressed in a makeshift robe with a towel around his head. Their faces glowed with wide smiles. "Hey, guys. You know I wouldn't want to miss my favorite nephew and niece's performance."

His nephew howled. "We're your only nephew and niece."

His niece raised her voice. "Uncle Ben, I'm going to be a lamb in the play."

"That's cool. What about your brother?"

"He's a shepherd."

"Well, I'm looking forward to the production." Ben glanced at Dave. "Where's your lovely wife?"

"She had to go early to help get the donuts and hot chocolate ready," his niece chimed in again.

Dave glanced in his rearview mirror. "You kids get quiet a minute so I can talk to Uncle Ben."

"Okay." The children drew out the word into two long syllables.

Dave chuckled. "Hey, man. See what you have in store someday. Fatherhood. Nothing can beat it." He turned into Fairville's main street through downtown.

Ben swallowed the lump in his throat. "Not planning on it anytime soon." That day was years off at the rate he was going. He hadn't had much luck with women yet.

"You never know. I didn't think I'd make it to the altar as soon as I did." Dave braked as the light turned red.

Not everyone was cut out for marriage. "Hey, lighten up." Ben gave his brother a friendly punch on the shoulder.

"Okay, okay." Dave stared straight ahead. "Not another word about your romantic life."

"Ha, ha. Which is non-existent."

Dave's church, Parkhill Christian, loomed ahead. Though Ben liked his brother's church, Willow Creek was closer to his apartment.

Dave pressed the gas pedal and headed down the street. "So, what you been up to lately?"

"Yesterday afternoon, I led a hike up to Prism Falls. We had an incident, but thankfully everything turned out fine."

"Oh?"

"One of the hikers tried to pet a black bear cub. Though she was a young teenager, she should've known better."

"Whoa. That's not good."

"I brought up the rear chatting with the girl while I watched for any danger. It was a good thing because she took off when she saw the cub. I wouldn't have seen the approaching mother bear had I not been right there."

"What did you do?"

"The old bear mace trick worked pretty well."

Dave glanced at Ben and back to the road again. "Do you like working as a state park ranger?"

Tightness in Ben's chest told him he didn't care to discuss the subject. But his brother deserved an answer. "It's okay. But not what I'd planned."

Dave frowned. "So, what happened?"

Saying the words was more painful than Ben thought. "After I graduated, I applied with the US Forestry Service. I had my eye on a job serving as a recreation and scenery resource specialist." He cleared his throat. "Didn't get the position."

Dave lowered his voice. "Awe man. You should've told me. I would've prayed for you."

"I know." Ben stuffed his hands in his jacket pockets. "I guess I didn't want to dwell on it. Besides, I'm thankful for the job with the Tennessee parks."

"Can you try again?"

"Maybe. It's very competitive and depends on what's available. But on the upside, I have some kind of drone job next week. The realty company I freelance for is sending me to Travisburg."

"I envy you there. Getting paid to play with remote controlled planes." Dave rolled his eyes.

"It's a little harder than that. But it's fun. And the extra money helps make ends meet." Ben turned around to the backseat. "Hey, kids. You've got a great dad.

He's my brother and also my friend." Ben chuckled under his breath. The adult Dave was a blessing. Different than the childhood Dave.

His brother pulled into the church parking lot and patted Ben's shoulder. "I'm proud of my little brother. Whether you get a different job or not. I want to see you try again one of these days."

"Thanks, I probably will." And he meant it. He opened the backseat door for his niece and nephew, and they piled out. "Okay, kids. Break a leg."

His niece's eyes grew wide. "You want us to get hurt?"

Ben chuckled. "No. That's only an expression. Let's go."

"Yes, Mom. I remember. I'm on my way now." Madison clicked off her phone, climbed into her car, and started the ignition. Her mom meant well, but sometimes she could act a little pushy. Madison didn't mind. She wanted to see tonight's children's Christmas performance at church anyway. After all, Mom was proud of being the director.

Madison turned out of her neighborhood onto Fairville's main street through the downtown section. The old part of town always displayed festive Christmas lights this time of year. She needed to get into the holiday spirit.

The Black Bear Inn appeared on her left, reminding her of yesterday's incident on the trail to Prism Falls. She still couldn't believe Ben hadn't prompted the rest of the group not to mess with the wildlife. He'd warned her and Melody at the orientation.

Ben.

Was he still the shy, little high school boy she'd always known? The guy who took twice as long as her to get anything done. When the group went out on photo shoots, he would wander off, taking closeups of plant life. Everyone had to wait on him because he lost track of time.

But that was in high school. Yesterday when he'd hung back proved to be a blessing. He'd handled the crisis like a professional, spraying the bear and keeping the creature at bay. He seemed to think more about the others than himself.

She shrugged and turned at the next street toward her family's church, the steepled building silhouetted in front of the setting sun. She never regretted being a member of Park Hills Christian Church along with her mom who directed the children's choir and the entire Montgomery family.

Inside, she made her way to the front as the fragrance of evergreens adorning the stage filled the sanctuary. A Christmas tree to the far left and a set depicting a living room complete with a hearth and stockings announced a holiday treat to the audience.

Madison took a seat in the second row. After several minutes, the house lights dimmed.

For the next hour, she lost herself in the celebration. A narrator told the story of Mary and Joseph and the baby Jesus born in Bethlehem while children wearing homemade costumes acted out the scriptures. Years ago, five-year-old Madison had paraded across the same stage dressed as a shepherd. Tonight, her heart swelled as she joined with the audience in singing, "Oh Come All Ye Faithful."

Finally, the entire cast of young actors and singers crowded the stage.

"Joy to the world, the Lord is come! Let earth receive her King. Let every heart prepare Him room. And heaven and nature sing."

With a bow, the kids returned to their parents in the audience.

Mom made her way to the stage. "Thank you for coming tonight. Have a glorious Christmas. And before you leave, please enjoy hot chocolate and spiced donuts in the fellowship hall."

Madison scooted out of the row and made her way to the side of the sanctuary. She fiddled with her cell phone to remove it from silent mode.

"Hey, Madison."

She glanced up at a towering guy in front of her. "Jacob Johnson. I remember you from high school."

"Yep. We were all a bunch of silly teenagers back then."

"You got that right." Madison gazed into hazel eyes peering at her. "I thought I saw you a couple of Sundays ago. How long have you been going to Parkhill Christian?"

"Only a few months." Jacob winked. "When I saw you one Sunday, I decided to stay."

Madison caught her breath and looked around at the crowd. What was she, an awkward teenager? Ridiculous. She turned to him again. "I'm glad you decided on this church. The pastor is a good teacher."

"In high school, I always wanted to ask you out but never got the nerve."

"We were all trying to figure things out then." Madison laughed. "I'm glad we don't have to live those days over again."

Jacob pulled his shoulders back and flashed a wide smile. "I may have been too shy in high school to ask you out, but I'm not any more. Wanta go for coffee sometime?"

Dating Jacob? Coffee wouldn't hurt, right? "Sure." Motion behind him caught Madison's attention.

Not more than three feet away from Jacob, a handsome guy with dark brown eyes approached and stopped. No doubt he'd heard most of their conversation.

She opened her mouth to say hello to Ben, but he stared at her for a moment, a question in his eyes. Then he walked away.

When Maddie glanced toward him, Ben stopped and then turned the other way. He wasn't hanging around while she seemed to be enthralled in conversation with some guy. A few steps toward the fellowship hall and he caught his shoe on the carpet covering the sanctuary floor. He stumbled forward like an out-of-control long jumper. His face warmed as if he'd smothered a nearby campfire. Hopefully she hadn't seen his awkward performance.

He continued to the room with the refreshments. His brother's kids had done a good job, and he needed to encourage them. He'd rather hang out with his family than see another second of Maddie's flirting.

Large evergreen branches were tied with red bows tacked up on the walls. A giant Christmas tree with blue and silver lights decorated one corner. He headed to the wide table laden with donuts, green and red cookies, iced cakes, and bowls of Christmas candy. At the end of the table, he filled a cup with hot chocolate from a large carafe.

Ben's niece and nephew charged toward him. "Did you like the show?"

"You guys did so well." He hugged them for a few seconds.

Later, Dave poked Ben's shoulder. "Ready to go?"

"Sure." He followed his brother, a kid on either side, out to the car. The drone job was coming up. Getting out of town would do him some good. At least he wouldn't run into Maddie.

Chapter Six

Monday morning, Madison finished her pumpkin spice latte and glanced at the email from her boss on her office computer.

"Need to see you in my office at nine to discuss an assignment. Get ready. This one may get you in the Christmas spirit. Kendrick."

Madison looked at the wall clock in her office at Cliffside Realty. Eight forty-five. Her messy desk held stacks of property releases and old photos. She dug around for her notebook where she recorded details of her assignments.

Her assignments—mostly routine. Maybe one day, she'd get a chance to use her imagination and create unique portraits of the Appalachian people.

Finally. Her small, blue spiral book appeared from under a pile of folders. She grabbed the notebook and headed out of her office. Turning to glance over her shoulder, she read the plaque on her door. Madison Montgomery, real estate photographer.

She lifted her chin and set out down the hall to Kendrick Grayson's office.

Photographer.

Not every real estate office hired a full-time person

to provide photos for brochures and clients. *Thank You, Lord, for my job.*

She tapped at the open door of Kendrick's office and stepped inside.

Her middle-aged boss' reading glasses rested on the end of his nose. He smoothed his mustache as he spoke to someone on the phone. Waving her in, he hung up his office landline receiver. "Come in, Madison."

Madison took a seat behind the large, L-shaped mahogany desk. "Your email intrigued me."

Kendrick snickered, picked up a manila folder, and thumbed through the papers. "I need you to drive down to Travisburg and shoot pictures of a large, historical property that we're handling for an Anabel Thatcher."

"Travisburg, the most popular tourist spot in our state? Wow."

Kendrick nodded. "The estate sits near Travisburg inside the northern edge of White Oak National Park. Mrs. Thatcher, the owner, is eight-two and can no longer manage this thirty-eight-acre property."

Madison widened her eyes. "I can understand why she needs to sell."

"Mrs. Thatcher has requested that our company list the house for sale."

Madison crossed one leg over the other. "Travisburg is a three-hour drive. When would I need to leave?"

"Wednesday morning. Hope that's not too soon." Kendrick glanced at his cell phone, paused, and then looked back at her. "Sorry. My secretary notified me the drone operator is here, and I want you to meet him." He passed her a folder. "Here's the information on the estate. I trust you to show the house in its best light and to present some great photos of the exterior and the outside property. I plan for you to be there through Friday. There's a lot of acreage for the drone to cover as well. You and the drone guy can drive together, if you'd like. I've booked two rooms at the Heidelberg Inn."

A tap sounded on the door. Maybe that was the free-lancer. Madison arose and picked up the folder. She took a few steps back. "All right. I'll go over the information."

Whack.

As if she'd made contact with a two-hundred-pound black bear, she caught her breath and turned.

A muscular guy reached to steady her. "Sorry. Are you okay?"

Madison opened her mouth and blinked her eyes. No. It couldn't be. "Ben. What are you doing here?"

"Madison, meet Ben Taylor. He's a freelance drone operator." Kendrick passed Ben a folder of information.

"M—M—Maddie? You're the photographer on the Thatcher property?"

Madison patted her chest as a cough rose in her throat. Ben? She hadn't seen him for two whole weeks. Now she had to spend two full days with him?

"Looks like you two already know each other. Sit down. I have some additional information for both of you." Kendrick pointed to the chairs.

Madison took a deep breath. Even the extra air in her lungs didn't relieve her angst. How was she supposed to work with Ben, the pseudo policeman who took it upon himself to maintain law and order with rock climbers? The guy whose unhurried pace drove her nuts. She'd never get anything done with him around. *Well, he better know his stuff and not slow her down.*

Kendrick continued. "The Thatcher estate was a mountain retreat of businessman Robert L. Vanderheim in the early nineteen hundreds. The buildings were made of natural materials such as hand-hewn logs and fieldstone. The man was a genius creating landscape features."

Ben sat up straight. "Hmm. Fascinating."

Kendrick glanced at Ben. "Landscape architecture. Wasn't that your college major?"

A bright smile appeared on Ben's face. "I hope to incorporate my degree into my park ranger job one of these days."

"Good deal." Kendrick looked at his watch. "Okay, folks. Back to your assignment. Most of the Vanderheim buildings have deteriorated except for the main house. This last year before the owner sells, she wants to create elaborate Christmas decorations in and out of the mansion and hold a Memory of Christmas event in the ballroom."

"I've read about it." Ben crossed his leg over his knee. "The Christmas ball was a big social event during the thirties and forties."

"True. I want you both to capture the beauty of the area, the magic of the seasonal décor, and landscape design of yesteryear. Our potential buyers need to see the decorated mansion, the property layout, any remaining landscape features and even the rundown structures to get an idea of the property's potential."

Madison laughed. "I love the challenge of an assignment like this." Though she thought she would've enjoyed making the trip with someone else, she couldn't wait to snap a pictorial record of Vanderheim's creative property design.

Kendrick lifted his index finger. "I haven't told you the most captivating aspect of the Thatcher property."

Madison smiled. "I'm listening."

Kendrick sat back in his chair, his hands clasped behind his head. "There are several mountain springs that flow through the property. You see, Vanderheim was fascinated with waterpower."

"That explains why he chose this site for his estate," Ben said.

"Yes. Get this," Kendrick held up a document, "rumor is that a springhouse they call The House of Fairies is built over one of the creeks. People have searched but no one has seen it for many years. It's almost as if it doesn't want to be found."

"But you'd like us to find it and get pictures?"

"Maybe it's a lot to ask, but that's why I'm giving you an extra day." Kendrick looked at Madison. "I hope you'll be able to locate it and get some shots of this elusive garden feature while you're there."

As if her insides were vibrating, Madison's pulse raced. "Incredible." She was headed to Travisburg for a mysterious pursuit of a house of fairies.

That afternoon, Ben stood on the sidewalk in front of Fairville's public library with his phone plastered to his ear. "Thanks, Mr. Wagner. I appreciate the time off. I'll be back by the weekend, so I could come in Saturday morning."

"Listen, Ben. Don't worry about coming in until after the holidays." His boss' voice rumbled. "Visits to the park have slowed due to the time of year. We got notice from the state to close down until after the new year. I was in the process of notifying all employees."

Ben made a fist pump. Time off to do a drone job excited him. Afterall, the work got him one step closer to the occupation he loved. "All right. Merry Christmas." Ben held open the library door for an elderly woman as she shuffled through, and then he veered off toward the local history section. After a few minutes, he pulled the volume he needed off the shelf.

Placing the reference book on the wooden table, he sank into the sturdy chair. He paged through until he found the right chapter. "The Vanderheim Estate—A Manmade Microcosm." Several pictures taken at the time Vanderheim lived there caught his attention. The property consisted of not only an estate, but workers' dwellings, barns, and a chicken hatchery. He flipped the page to another diagram. There were numerous gardens and a springhouse. And an old black and white photo of the place Kendrick told them about, The House of Fairies.

He closed his eyes and allowed his imagination to go to work. Walking through a dense forest, Ben climbed the rocky stairs. At the top, the barrel-vault constructed springhouse appeared. He walked closer. Through an open door, he saw them. Fireflies the reference book described as fairies. Flittering, sparkling, flashing their lights.

A few moments later, he opened his eyes and gazed around at the vast array of bookshelves. He had to hand it to himself. His imagination was active. Well, in only a few days, he'd see the fairy house as it looked today, that is if they could find it.

Now to call Maddie and tell her he'd take his car.

The evening after her meeting with her boss, Madison punched her mom's speed dial button. "Hey, Mom."

"Hey, honey. I'm so glad you came to the performance Sunday."

"Are you kidding? I wouldn't want to miss it. You do a great job with those kids."

Mom's tone brightened. "I appreciate that, and I'm looking forward to our family Christmas celebrations."

"Me, too. That's why I called. I'm leaving Wednesday on a job assignment to Travisburg. It's a two-day project so I should be back Friday afternoon. Since Christmas is the next week, I'll have plenty of time to help out with whatever you need."

"That's a great place to go this time of year with all the festive lights and decorations."

"Have you heard of the Vanderheim estate?"

"Yes. Your father was friends of one of the carpenters the owner hired to work on the mansion. We visited Travisburg on our honeymoon and were able to drive over to the estate to tour the grounds."

Madison paced to her living room windows and back. "Part of my boss' assignment is to capture a picture of hidden springs around the property."

"What a challenge. You drive carefully, sweetie."

"Only downside is, I'm going with that guy I knew

from high school, Ben Taylor. Do you remember him?"

"Vaguely. I think you mentioned his name a few times." Mom chuckled. "Never in a good context, though. Take my advice and make the best of things."

The best of things? She'd have to overlook a lot of Ben's annoying habits.

Chapter Seven

Ben carefully placed his flight bag with his drone in the cargo area of his four-wheel drive next to his duffle bag flares and first aid kit. Hopefully Maddie wouldn't have too much equipment. He'd taken up most of the back area. Closing the hatch, he started the ignition.

Surprising how close Madison's apartment was to his, something he hadn't realized until she gave him her address Monday. He turned at the red light, pulled up to the curb in front of her place, and did a double take.

Maddie stood on the sidewalk with a mound of equipment, her foot moving up and down like a tap dancer, her arms folded over her chest.

He glanced at his watch. Only five minutes late. That woman mystified him.

He jumped out of the car. "Let me help you load your gear." She'd no doubt come prepared with the cameras, lenses, tripods, and lighting equipment. Guess he couldn't fault her for that.

She lifted her hand in a stop position. "Hold on. I'll do my own packing." She marched toward her equipment and glanced at the open cargo area. Then she glared at him. "Where am I supposed to put my load if your back area is full?"

"Look, Maddie. I can fold down the back seat and there'll be plenty of room. Put your tripod in first." If he'd ever seen a high-strung woman, Maddie was a perfect example.

"Okay." No smile on her face, she stuffed the rest of her things in his car and crawled into the passenger seat, again wrapping her arms around her middle.

Ben pulled onto the main road to Travisburg. If Maddie didn't lighten up a bit, this might be a long two days. Well, he needed to concentrate on his work most of all.

As they left town, Ben cleared his throat. "I read up on the area a little more yesterday at the library."

For the first time today, Maddie's expression changed, and she smiled. "I really want to get some shots of the springhouse Kendrick spoke about."

"How did you get into real-estate photography? A far stretch from nature and portrait work."

"Taking pictures of people and places is an amazing creative outlet. Experimenting with different lighting, places, and unusual backdrops. But it doesn't pay the bills."

He got it. "So, you put your skills to work in commercial photography?"

Her laugh reminded him of the bell-like sounds of his wind chimes on his apartment's balcony. "I thought I'd go into the work full time and enjoy the creative side on the weekends. Maybe one day I'll put something together and place my material online."

He relaxed as he gripped the steering wheel. "I have a strong feeling you'll do it, too."

"Thanks, Ben. I appreciate the support." Maddie

crossed her legs.

As they gained elevation, Ben flipped on the car heater. "That ok? We're going to see some snow. I'm glad I've got winter tires on my Jeep."

Maddie withdrew fuzzy gloves from her large carrying bag. "I think you're right. Those little fluffy crystals are beginning to accumulate on your windshield. What about you, Ben? Do you like your job?"

"I'm thankful for the work, but sometimes it's frustrating. I'm like you. I wish I had the chance to be more creative. I would love to get involved with the design of the park instead of law enforcement."

After thirty minutes, the wipers rotated back and forth at top speed, barely clearing the snow accumulation. Ben slowed the car. No sense in skidding off the road. Better to be late and arrive safely than not arrive at all.

Maddie looked at her smart watch and frowned. "We're running behind. I hate to miss out on needed daylight hours."

Ben rolled his eyes. "Maddie, we need to get there safely."

Maddie rolled down her window, sniffed the air, and rolled it up again. She looked at the sky. "The open fields have disappeared. Nothing but dense forest lining the road now. I can barely see the evergreens. They look like a haze of white smoke."

Ahead, the road took a curve to the right. Ben gripped the steering wheel tighter and started the turn. As if the car had a mind of its own, the vehicle continued forward crossing the oncoming lane and crashed into something hard, bringing the auto to an

abrupt stop on the opposite side of the road.
Maddie grasped her throat and screamed.

Chapter Eight

Ben took a deep breath, turned off the motor, and glanced at the nervous woman by his side. "Wait here. I'll check to see if there's any damage." He prayed they hadn't run so far into a snowbank that they'd need to be towed out.

Maddie scrunched down into her seat. "Now, we're going to be even later."

Resisting the urge to say something he shouldn't, he stepped outside the car. He placed one foot into the snow and then the other, taking unhurried steps. He clenched his jaw. The Jeep had collided with a large rock bending the rim on the front right tire which deflated quickly. No driving on the tire now.

He jumped into the driver's seat. "The good news is we're not stuck in a snowbank, but I'm going to have to change the tire."

"Why did you run off the road like that?"

Ben filled his cheeks and blew the air out in a slow stream. "I didn't do it on purpose, Maddie. I believe the problem was the tires lost traction. Must've hit an ice patch. The right tire is blown."

Ben dug in his glove compartment and pulled out a small object. "Here." He placed the small portable car heater in the cup holder on her side and pressed the button behind the fan. "This should keep you warm while the car is off."

She blinked a couple of times as if his gesture surprised her. "Thanks."

The spare tire hung on the back cargo door, but the jack sat under mats in the rear. He pulled out a couple of bags and laid them on the frozen ground exposing the jack's storage location. Finally, he lifted the car jack from its hiding spot and set out to change the tire.

Flakes of freezing snow landed on his nose and cheeks. Twenty minutes later, the job complete, and everything back in place, he returned to the car and got in.

Maddie pounded her cell phone's screen and glanced up at him. "Awesome. We're good to go now."

He caught his breath as a ray of sunlight sparkling through the trees and onto the clean white of the mountainside looked like miniature diamonds twinkling in the air. "Would you like to snap a picture of the frozen world out here? It's exquisite."

"Better not. We're behind schedule as it is now." She gave a quick shake of her head.

Ben took one more glance at the glorious scene of nature God had created. If he had his way, Maddie would slow down and enjoy life a bit.

Madison had to hand it to Ben. He was prepared. She'd seen the extra emergency equipment in back, and it didn't take him long to change the tire. And the heater. Even so, they might not have much time to look around the area when they made it to Travisburg as they had an hour's drive before them.

Ben stared at the winding road as he gripped the steering wheel and slowed at the icy patches.

Why hadn't she studied his handsome profile before? "How did you get into flying drones?"

Ben looked at her and back at the road again. "You know how kids are. I used to play with drones. Later after I got interested in photography, I learned how to incorporate both skills into a parttime profession."

Madison caught her breath. "To see what a bird sees with those aerial shots. Thrilling."

"I could teach you if you want. Some of the new machines almost fly themselves."

Sure, but he must've had problems when he first started. "Have you ever crashed one?"

"Oh, yeah. I've sent a few to the ground." Ben smirked. "When we get to Travisburg, I could run into problems with the cold temps. Below freezing and my battery will go fast. That means the controls won't function as they should. You know, a bit wonky."

"Wonky? Is that a word your grandmother uses?" She rubbed her temple. Ben was different from the other men she knew, almost as if he were from another time.

Ben removed his heavy scarf from around his neck in the warm car. The outskirts of Travisburg appeared in the distance. "Almost there." He caught a glance of

Maddie.

She thumbed through the screen on her cell phone. "This picture of Melody the day Andy led us on the climb turned out well." Her voice quiet, she reflected an enthusiasm he hadn't heard before.

"Have you been rock climbing long?"

"I joined a climbing gym about three years ago. Then a couple of friends invited me on an outdoor climb. I was hooked. Every chance I get I'm out there. No matter what's going on in life, challenging myself on the rock helps put everything in perspective." Maddie leaned forward in her seat.

"Andy said you were good. That makes sense, you climb a lot."

"So, you and Andy were talking about me?" Maddie raised one eyebrow.

"It—it wasn't like that." Ben held his breath to control the nervous laugh.

Travisburg's downtown came into view. He better go to the repair shop and get the tire fixed before going to the hotel. Since Travisburg was a small town, he prayed they hadn't shut down for the holiday season. He wouldn't want to drive back home without a spare.

Madison pulled out her cell phone. "I'll put the Heidelburg Inn in my GPS. When we get our suitcases into our rooms, we may have time to drive over to the Vanderheim property before it gets late."

"Can you do me a favor and check for tire repair shops?" Ben smiled. "We need to take a detour first." Responsibility for them both weighed on him. "I need to get the tire repaired."

Maddie lifted her voice an octave. "We don't have time for that."

"Look, Maddie. I'm sorry, but first things first."

"Men," she muttered. "You take time to notice the trees when you're changing a tire. I'm trying to keep us on schedule."

"True. But I also need to protect ..." He'd begun to say *you* but couldn't give her the idea he might see her as more than a colleague? "I—I—I need to get us both back safely to Fairville in a couple of days."

She nodded. "I suppose you're right."

After ten more minutes, Ben pulled up in front of an automotive service that popped up on Maddie's GPS—Bubba's Tire Repair. "I'll be back." He retrieved the damaged tire from the back and rolled it inside the building. After leaving it with the employee, he returned to give Maddie the report.

"How'd it go?" She peered at him as he slipped into the driver's seat.

"Not good news. We have a problem. Two employees didn't show up today, so we won't have our repair until morning."

"That will put us a half day behind schedule." Maddie folded her arms. "But I guess we have no choice."

"The shop opens at eight and our tire should be ready by nine. I checked my phone. The drive from here to the Heidelberg isn't far. The weather should clear up by tomorrow."

He hoped the sun would come out earlier rather than later in the morning. He couldn't afford to have problems with his drone. And he couldn't disappoint his boss—or Maddie.

Chapter Nine

Madison opened the blinds in her spacious room at the Heidelburg. The cloudy sky darkened as the sun set. Snow blanketed the trees, bushes on the hotel's property, and the street. Few cars drove on the roadway—as if the population of Travisburg, Tennessee had gone into hibernation. For a moment, Fairville, in the foothills of the Donald Gap State Park, seemed far away as this frozen hamlet now became reality.

Madison picked up her phone and punched in her friend's number.

"Hey." Melody sounded like she was finishing up a bite of something. "How's your photo job going?"

"That's why I called—to tell you what happened. We had a problem on the way up. A flat tire." She combed her fingers through her hair. "Now we don't have enough time—nor good weather, to check out the Vanderheim property today. If the elements don't clear up by tomorrow, we might not be able to finish the job, and our trip to Travisburg could be a failure."

Melody guffawed. "You don't want to get snowed in with the hunky guy, either."

"Ha. I hope that doesn't happen."

"Okay, girlfriend. Praying for you."

"Thanks. I appreciate that." Madison looked around for her suitcase. She rummaged through her clothes to the bottom for her earmuffs. The merino wool shirt she'd strewn on the side of the bed would be a good underlayer. Ben said he wanted to go for a walk later and to meet him for dinner in the Heidelburg dining room. Best German food in town, the sign at the restaurant entrance had said. Then afterward, he wanted to take a walk around downtown Travisburg. Brr. She'd better bring every warm item of clothing she had.

Ben.

She closed her eyes a moment. She had to admit his square jaw and broad shoulders were attractive. Okay, he was downright handsome. If only he weren't so shy and structured with his life. But she had gotten him talking when she asked him about drones. What else was he interested in?

Maddison grabbed her coat and headed out to the elevator. She punched *two* for the floor to the restaurant—Bonhoffer's Schnitzel Haus. When the doors glided open, Ben waited, one arm resting on the ledge of the tall European window.

A half smile on his face, he glanced down at her, his dark eyes twinkling. "Glad you could finally make it."

She gave him a playful swat and ignored her increased heart rate. The high altitude got to her, she was sure. She giggled. "I usually have to wait on you while you look at the scenery."

His laugh rumbled, a soothing sound she enjoyed. He patted his stomach. "I'm starved. Can't wait to dive into one of those breaded Schnitzels with home fried potatoes."

The hostess showed them to a spot near the window. "This okay?" She set two menus down on the table.

"Great." Ben rushed around to Madison's side to hold her chair.

Madison's eyes widened. She'd never have figured Ben would act like a gentleman. "Thanks."

Outside the window, shops with closed signs lined the other side of the road. A tall street lamp wrapped with a red and white ribbon shed light along the sidewalk.

"Still up for a walk after dinner?" Ben picked up his menu.

"Sounds great." Surprising he didn't irritate her as much as he had earlier today. "You told me how you got into drones. But why work with the real estate company? Does the Tennessee Park system mind you moonlighting?"

"They're usually flexible with my schedule." Ben's jaw tightened.

Had she hit on a sore subject? Madison turned to the long list of Schnitzels.

An hour later and dinner finished, Ben ordered two slices of apfelkuchen, the German version of apple cake. She had to admit, though they'd gotten off to a slow start, being in Travisburg in the snowy weather with Ben wasn't as bad as she'd thought.

She finished the yellow, crumbly cake with sliced apples and powdered sugar on top. "I need to work this delicious meal off."

Ben placed his napkin on the table. "Ready for that walk?"

"Any other time, I'd say you're crazy to go out in this freezing weather, but now, definitely."

The globe lights illuminated the snow-covered streets and the mountain in the distance that probably featured ski runs. Maddie buttoned up her down filled coat and donned her wool gloves and earmuffs. Her fur-lined boots she rarely had opportunity to wear would come in handy tonight in the winter wonderland.

On the main street lit with strings of Christmas lights, they turned up a road to the left.

"This way to the river which runs through the town." Streams of smoke curled from Ben's mouth as he spoke. "I like to come up here fishing in the summer."

"Not this time of year, though."

"Generally, no, but the water isn't frozen."

A bridge came into view spanning the wide Travisburg River as it gurgled with the flow. Archways covered with red and green lights decorated the walkway. Madison gasped. Lighted structures resembling sparkling, silver trees lined the sides of the path. Was she walking through a magic passageway to the other side? She giggled at her silly thoughts.

Ben paused at a section of the metal fencing at the top of the bridge and rested his arms as he gazed into the water.

Across the way, the illumination from a brightly lit building mirrored sparkles of light onto the rolling river.

He chuckled. "At the library, I read about the phenomenon of fireflies in the area. The reflections on the moving water reminds me of the little creatures."

Madison propped her arms on the railing next to

Ben. He was right. The colorful, gently moving river was stunning.

Ben turned to her. "I know you're concerned about completing the project on time, but we'll make it." He patted her mitten. "Don't worry."

Madison stood straight and faced him. "You know, Ben, you've changed a lot since high school. I admit, I sat back and didn't say anything when my friends gave you a hard time." Why was she becoming so honest with him?

He caught her gaze. "I'll be truthful with you. I'm sorry I teased you about your red curls." He reached to push a strand of her hair out of her face and gave her a shy smile. "I only did it to get your attention."

Madison couldn't break her gaze. She read it in his expression. He meant those words.

Had Ben really confessed his boyish mindset to her? These days he'd matured and walked on from those childish ways. Fine. Then what more adult strategies did he know to cultivate a better relationship—maybe a connection that went beyond friendship?

He cleared his throat. Better move on. "The town center is a block on the other side of the river. Wanta go? I'd like to take a look at the landscape design."

A red brick walkway lined with old fashioned streetlights steered them to the main plaza. In the center a small fountain, dripping with icicles, sat surrounded by raised flower beds. The winter pansies peeked through newly fallen snow. "It usually doesn't get that cold here. They keep flowers growing year-round. If it were me, I'd put in more evergreen plants."

Madison smiled. "I see the landscape architect shining through."

His face warmed, shooing away the cold for a moment. Had she begun to change her opinion of him?

They strolled past the fountain to a gazebo strung with lights, so bright that the surrounding area looked like day. Several pine trees off to the side shadowed a bright red sleigh.

"The Christmas lights are spectacular." Maddie turned her head from side to side, probably taking everything in.

"This gazebo is lit up even in the summer." Ben led them to a brick bench built into a retaining wall. "The landscaping is beautiful, but they should feature more plants native to the area."

"Seems like you notice everything." Maddie's eyes twinkled.

"Maybe if you weren't in such a hurry all the time, you would see a few things too."

Her smile faded as quickly as a spent sparkler.

Ben tightened his jaw. The last thing he wanted to do was tick her off. But then if two people couldn't be honest with each other, how could they ever sustain a friendship? He tapped his head. Women? Would he ever understand them?

They walked in silence back to the hotel. At the elevator, Maddie punched her floor and glanced at him. "Let's make it early, tomorrow."

Ben got out of the lift on the next floor and ambled down the hall to his room. Face it. The possibility of a relationship with Maddie looked bleak—not even a decent friendship.

Chapter Ten

Ben peered at Maddie over his menu. The aromas in the hotel's breakfast room made him hungry. The smoky, meaty smell of bacon, pancakes with the scent of darkened flour, brown sugar, and butter, and the caramelized, nutty aroma of coffee brewing. "Sh—sh—shall I say the blessing?"

She nodded. "Please do."

When Ben slipped his large hand over Maddie's smaller one, his heart decided to pound a few beats faster. What was that about? "Lord, thank You for the breakfast we are about to eat. Allow us to accomplish the work we need to finish today."

Maddie lifted her face and blinked, her lips parted.

What was that expression? Ben had no idea.

After the server filled his cup with steaming coffee, Ben added a dash of cream and sipped a taste. The dark, woodsy brew provided the extra portion of stamina he needed to operate the drone and complete their project today.

Maddie looked over his shoulder to the windows on the other side of the room. "The weather looks like it may cooperate. The blue skies will make our job easier."

"Soon as we finish breakfast, we can retrieve the tire and head out to the Vanderheim property." Ben moved his napkin into his lap when the server set a large plate of blueberry pancakes, butter melting on top, and a pitcher of hot maple syrup in front of him.

Maddie took a bite of her crispy bacon. "I can't wait to get an idea of the layout of the property. And hunt for the springhouse."

Ben spread the butter on top of his pancake. "I'm anxious to see the springhouse for myself. I read a little about it last week at the Fairville Library." He took a bite of pancakes and swallowed. "The structure is built over a bubbling spring. Inside, the temperature stays cool in warm weather so the first owners, the Vanderheims, used it to store food."

Maddie patted her mouth with her napkin. "You mean like a refrigerator?"

"Yes, and the springhouse also kept the water clean from falling debris. But my favorite part about the springhouse is the fireflies. In the summer, even to this day, they come out of hibernation. At night the springhouse looks like it's inhabited by a flutter of fairies with their flashing, glowing lights."

Maddie snapped her fingers. "Since this is winter, I guess we won't be able to see them."

Ben gave her a mischievous smile. "I wouldn't be so sure about that."

Her eyes widened. "Why?"

"There's a legend that at Christmastime, the spring delivers spurts of warm water. With it, the fireflies emerge from hibernation for a while and grace the opening of the springhouse with their presence. Voila. The fairies return."

Maddie clapped her hands. "Do you suppose we'll see the phenomenon?"

"We'll have to walk through a forest and climb rocky stairs to get to the Vanderheim springhouse built into the side of the mountain."

"But first, we'll have to locate the general area."

Ben smiled. "Yep. Mr. Vanderheim built it somewhere on the property, so if we don't give up, we may be able to find the structure."

Madison stared out the window of Ben's car. She lifted her Nikon to get a shot of the snowy mountains creating a backdrop for the quaint buildings of downtown Travisburg, many adorned with wreaths, bulbs, and silver lights strung from the rooftops and windows.

Ben pulled up in front of the tire shop and went in.

Madison tugged her jacket around her and crossed her fingers. The tire just had to be ready. The Vanderheim estate waited to be explored. She couldn't ask for a better assignment—hiking, hunting for fairy houses, and shooting photos of an enormous estate adorned with Christmas lights.

Then she remembered breakfast when Ben placed his hand on hers to pray. Tingles had raced up her arm. What happened? Was the reaction the result of a growing attraction to Ben? She might feel drawn to him, but they were both so different. Ben, serious, and closed like a bolted vault. He'd never let her in—if she wanted a place in his heart.

Ben strolled out of the shop, rolling the tire along the sidewalk.

She glanced in the rearview mirror as Ben hoisted the tire into the storage rack. From the sound of a slam, she figured he bolted the latch.

He stepped into the car. "We can be on our way now. I'm anxious to get some good drone shots of the property today. I'd like to capture aerial shots of the thirty-eight acres and then videos of specific places in the area."

Madison's heart skipped a beat. She loved an adventure as much as Ben.

Madison gripped her hands in her lap as Ben maneuvered the narrow, curving road to the Vanderheim estate. "Is that the turn in?" She pointed ahead.

"Yes. Finally. This fog didn't help much." Ben steered off Apple Orchard Road onto the narrow rock-covered drive. Tall pines lined the road.

After a few twists on the route, a flat, wooden bridge with no railings appeared. Boulders lay in the middle of the riverbed, no doubt swept there by last summer's rains. "Let's hope this structure is sound. The stream underneath is only a trickle."

"We'll be fine." Ben glanced out his window.

Glad *he* was confident. After crossing the water, the land opened up to acres that once had been cleared for the homes, gardens and orchards of the late Mr. Vanderheim. Sunshine broke through the pines chasing the mist away.

As they arrived at the mansion, Madison caught her breath. The fieldstone walls of the two-story manor appeared to grow out of the ground. Exiting the car, they trekked toward the building with its rich brown chestnut shingles topped by the pointed roof. Madison strolled onto a long, covered porch as Ben held the dark oak door.

Her eyes adjusted as she entered the spacious lounging area. A gray-haired woman in a trim black skirt, pale yellow bouse, and heels walked toward them. "Good morning. I'm Janice Maddox, the representative for Mrs. Anabel Thatcher."

"Yes, Anabel, the owner." Madison pulled out her business card and handed it to the woman. "We're here representing Cliffside Realty in Fairville. We're on assignment to take aerial and ground photographs of the property."

Ms. Maddox extended her hand. "Ms. Thatcher said you'd probably be here today. If you need anything, please ask."

Madison looked up at the large map on the wall near the entrance, took a photo with her cell phone, and retrieved her notebook containing the list of structures.

Mrs. Maddox pointed to the map. "This is the entire property. I have a smaller version I will give you."

Setting her camera bag on the polished wood floor, Madison glanced toward the map. "We understand that a number of the building have fallen into disrepair, but we still plan to photograph them."

"Yes, at one time Mr. Vanderheim developed this area into a self-sufficient community. His family ate food from the gardens and orchards."

Ben stepped closer and cleared his throat. "I read that there were several barns for cows and horses and a chicken hatchery." He pointed above the house on the map. "Are they up here?"

"Yes. Mr. Vanderheim created hydroelectric power which ran the whole property so they were heated and lighted. The locals laughed at Vanderheim and called his barns palaces."

"What about the gardens?" Madison slipped her pen behind her ear. "We've heard that there are areas that have been lost."

"Mr. Vanderheim was a man of unending energy." Ms. Maddox lifted her shoulders, her face reflecting her admiration for the family. "He employed several workmen from the surrounding area—at good wages, I might add. There's a spring somewhere on that hill." She motioned to the left on the other side of the bridge they crossed. "He built a springhouse right over the bubbling underground water. Then he terraced it with native stones so that the brook would fall over the rocks descending into a pool below. The family loved to swim there."

Madison held her breath as Ms. Maddox continued the story.

"Next to the springhouse on the uppermost terrace is a tiny flight of stairs leading to a doll-sized castle. One of the workers built it. The story is, when Vanderheim asked him what it was for, he explained that it was for the fairies. Since then, the springhouse has been called the Fairy House."

"We'd love to see it." Ben's eyes sparkled, and he rubbed his hands together.

"I wish I could tell you where it is." Ms. Maddox

shook her head. "But I only have the stories."

"What about Ms. Thatcher? Has she or members of her family made an attempt to find the springhouse?" Ben said.

"I can't tell you, but I'm sure in recent years, she hasn't. At least not after her husband died, and her health has declined as of late."

"Perhaps the fairy house is merely a fictious tale passed down through the years?" Madison reached for the copies of the map the other woman gave her and passed one to Ben.

Ms. Maddox gave them a playful smile. "No, I've seen pictures from Ms. Thatcher's collection which she claims were taken of the place."

Madison smiled. "All right, then. Thank you for your help."

"Call me Janice. And please be careful as you walk around. Snow may have covered loose rocks."

Where to start? She could photograph the main house tomorrow before they left. Today, she'd shoot some of the outbuildings. And who knew? Maybe they'd discover the mysterious springhouse.

Chapter Eleven

Ben peered at Maddie as she seemed to flit to one place to another, like a butterfly. That woman displayed more energy than a boxer training for a match. She moved from the horse barn in disrepair to the chicken hatchery to the orchard which had become overgrown with weeds and grass.

On the path into the woods, she slowed and pounded on her cell phone.

"What cha doing? I thought you were in a hurry."

"I'm answering the text from Melody, my climbing friend. She was asking how the job was going today."

"Good. I need to stop for a moment, anyway, to get my drone in operation. This will take a little time to get set up."

She waved. "Sure thing." She walked nearer. "I'm interested in how you operate that thing."

Ben's chest swelled. Sure, he wanted to show her. He set his equipment bag on the wide ledge of a stone wall that no doubt dated back to when Vanderheim originally built his estate and grounds. He lifted the drone from his equipment bag and then the controls.

"Okay, first I turn on the drone." He held up the silver and black device. "Then the control propellers.

I'll do a hand launch this time." He waved at Maddie. "Please stand over by that rock wall. I don't want you to get hurt."

The controls in his right hand and the drone in his left, he launched his machine toward the breeze blowing from the north. "I'm performing aerial videography to give us a perspective of the entire property. Later I'll do some still photography."

Instead of standing out of the way, Maddie looked over his shoulder as Ben watched the images on his phone—the wooden bridge on which they drove in, the weed-ridden gardens and the main house, a creek meandering into the area from the bordering mountain, and finally the woods close to where they stood now. "The Fairy House must be somewhere on that creek. We're near the area where hikers explore in search of the fairy house."

"Really?" Maddie's eyes widened. "Where did you hear that?"

"I told Andy what we were doing. He said he'd heard hikers talking about it."

"Have any of them found the springhouse?"

"No, unfortunately." He looked toward the hills. "What do you say we give it a go since we're here? You can get some good shots of the woods, and if we find the house of the fairies, you'd no doubt get a raise." He gave a loud guffaw.

Maddie's face lit in a wide smile. "Yeah, good idea." Then she glanced at her smartwatch, and the grin disappeared. "I don't think we can. We spent a lot of time shooting the outbuildings."

Ben lifted his brow. "Imagine how impressed your boss would be if we found the house. Besides, don't you want to see the mysterious place?"

Maddie poked out her lip and nodded her head. "Okay, if we haven't found it in the next hour, I'm coming back to the main area."

"You got it." Ben landed the drone. "I'll fly it again in a bit so we'll have a visual of where we're going."

"Okay, let's hurry up." Maddie hoisted her camera bag on her shoulder and set out toward the woods.

Ben followed her over a narrow bridge spanning a gurgling creek and into a stand of silvery, bare trees with a mountain range beyond. With the woods to the north and smaller hills and trees south of them, would they discover the fairy house built into the side of one of those hills?

Madison stomped through dried and dead grass avoiding the piled snow farther into the trees. Were they lost?

Ben.

Why was he so relaxed? Didn't he sense deadlines and time limits? Well, she supposed they could take an hour out today. Besides, if they discovered the fairy house and she got shots of the springhouse, she *would* impress her boss. Who knew? Maybe her photos would make the news.

"Slow down, Maddie. I'm launching the drone." Like a dragonfly, the machine rose and hovered. He traced the path with his finger on the video feed. "See, here's the creek that winds around that bend. The stream disappears into those trees. We should head in that direction."

Glancing at her watch, Maddie picked up her pace and followed the brook. "I want to find the springhouse before the sun goes down. Why do we have to always be so slow and lumbering? It drives me crazy. Just get the work done, Ben. That's what we came here to do."

He gawked at her for a moment and then shook his head. "You haven't changed, have you? Well, yeah, you have. It used to be your friends that made the cruel remarks. I thought maybe you thought differently and just stayed quiet. Seems they were always on the tip of your pointed tongue."

How dare he? She'd never been cruel to him. Yes, her friends had, but that hadn't been her. "Catch up with me when you can." She turned.

"No. No. No. Wait, Maddie. My drone crashed into a tree at the edge of those woods." He pointed toward the north. "Come with me to recover the equipment, and then we can continue the search."

Frustration rose in Madison's chest. They didn't have the time for that. "No. You go on and catch up with me after you find your drone, if you can catch up with me."

"What's that supposed to mean?" Ben frowned. "I may need your help."

Maddie blew out a stream of air. "No, I'm going on. You've wasted too much time already." She turned to glare at him.

He shook his head. "You haven't changed at all."

She tightened her fists. "And what is *that* supposed to mean?"

"You may never have been outright cruel to me, but you stood alongside those who were, and it was cruel,

Maddie. You had to have known how much I cared for you." He turned and started in the opposite direction.

Had she really seemed mean to him all those years ago in high school? And he'd cared for her? No time to think now. Madison picked up her pace as she trekked further into the woods. She wrapped her scarf around her neck against the breezy day. His words replayed in her head.

Had she agreed with her friends so long ago and simply stayed quiet to let them be the mean ones? She narrowed her eyes. Why had she stayed quiet?

She'd been afraid of losing their friendship?

But what about Ben? Couldn't he have used a friend?

Would he have been a better friend, making her a better person?

After fifteen minutes, the quiet gurgling of the stream, like an orchestra tuning up for a concert, became louder. Water tumbled over the watermelon sized boulders. She walked parallel along the side of the creek up an incline. Was she close? The information had said the springhouse was built on the side of a hill.

The wind blew harder as she continued up the incline. Water flowed over terraced ledges forming pools in the stream bed as Janice had described. Madison paused at a set of partially crumbling rock steps sliding off the path like slow moving glaciers. Ferns crowded around them. Her heart pounded. Could the fairy house be nearby?

A structure like a retaining wall jutted to the right, and the steps continued up the mountain. Madison breathed harder as she climbed more and more steps, each wet with the mist and layers of moss creeping up from the sides.

Deep croaking and a whirling noise made Madison jump. She balanced with two arms in the air as her foot threatened to slip off the rock. A common raven flapped his wings and glided to another tree with a guttural protest. She'd invaded his territory.

Finally, after more steps, a small rock building, arched like a sliced barrel, emerged from the side of the mountain. The front and curved roof were covered with deep green moss and lime colored lichen. Madison's heart pounded out of her chest. Was this the fairy house?

She raced the rest of the way and glanced inside the structure. The stones in the center of the room opened revealing a three-foot wide space. Water from the pool flowed down a channel under the floor and out of the building. Was that steam rising from the water? Madison held her hand closer. The bubbling water radiated heat. The water was warm but no fireflies.

She clasped her chest, took another deep breath, and then readied her camera for a shot. After snapping a few, she glanced at her watch. Where was Ben? He needed to see this. For sure, she'd found the fairy house.

That guy. He was never in a hurry.

Stashing away her Nikon, she turned to rush down the stairs again. As if walking on ice, her foot slid on the moss, and she lost her balance. Her camera bag flew into the air rolling under a bush. Pain split the side of her head. Darkness overtook her.

Chapter Twelve

Madison groaned as she rubbed her forehead.

A tiny face stared at her. The eyes, blue as sapphires opened wide, unblinking. The creature hung in the air as her long translucent wings fluttered, the speed causing flashes of light. She darted away as another with golden hair dipped down. Then there were three, spinning around as if playing tag, their dresses pale— teal, pink, and lavender. The hum of their wings sang a tune, high as the notes of a flute, growing louder and then suddenly, quiet, and they were gone.

Madison pushed against the rock step and sat up. Strange. The stone didn't feel slippery any more but dry and smooth. Maybe moss hadn't grown over each of them.

Pain in the side of her forehead told her she'd fallen against something—perhaps one of the stone steps. She touched the side of her head to find a warm, sticky substance.

Opening her eyes, she glanced around. The same silvery winter trees surrounded her. Some of the dead limbs she'd seen on the forest floor seemed to have disappeared. How long had she been unconscious? Where was Ben? She lifted her hand to peer at gooey, red blood coating her fingers.

As if her thoughts had conjured him, Ben rushed toward her, helping her to sit up the rest of the way. "Madam, are you all right?" Ben's eyes were wide, and he wore a deep frown. "You've received an injury."

"Ben." Madison scrubbed her eyes harder.

He wore a black hat with a wide brim and overalls.

"Did you change clothes? Where did you get that weird hat? I've never seen you wear it before."

Ben stared at her as if she'd lost her mind. "Ma'am, my name is Benjamin. But how did you know my nickname that only my mother uses?"

She blinked. Something did seem different about him.

"Ben, quit acting so strange and help me up." She wasn't sure what kind of joke he was playing, but she didn't care for it at all. She held out her arm for him to give her a boost up.

"You obviously have taken a fall. You must stand up slowly." Ben frowned but supported her as she got to her feet. Again, he looked at her as if he'd seen a ghost. "Might I ask, why you're in the forest and wearing men's trousers?"

Madison adjusted the sleeves of her hoodie and brushed leaves off her jeans. "Okay, Ben. I've had enough. No more joking around. Did you find your drone?"

Ben pressed his lips together in a grimace. "I'm sure I don't know to what you are referring." He glanced around the forested area. "I think you need help. I'll take you up to the main house. Perhaps we can call the doctor."

Madison took a few wobbly steps, and then her

head spun.

"Oh, my." Benjamin wrapped his arms around her and lowered her to sit on the ground against a small retaining wall a few steps away. "Stay here. I'm going for help." Ben lifted his hat off his head, wiped his forehead with a handkerchief, and plopped it on again. He raced down the hill and stopped.

"Benjamin." A man in a baggy-looking suit with a tie and a hat ran toward them.

The man's suit reminded her of the kind of clothing gangsters wore in an old movie she saw once. *Scarface.*

"I was out for my morning walk and heard voices." Baggie suit eyed Madison and then glanced at Ben. "Do you need help?"

"Yes, sir. I finished planting the tulips and daffodil bulbs in the gardens around the mansion and also took a walk. I came across a strange woman on the steps at the springhouse."

Madison's pulse raced. So, she *had* found the springhouse.

The man in the suit took deliberate steps toward her and stopped. He tilted his face from one side to the other, staring at her as if she were a creature from outer space. "Here, together we can get her up to the estate. Dr. Dankworth can drive right over."

Madison pushed up using the stone wall to help her stand. Again, dizziness overtook her, and she yielded to the support of the two men.

They walked out of the woods the way she and Ben had come—through the forest, over the bridge, and past the orchard. A bit wobbly, she clung to the guys on either side of her.

Taking a rapid, second look, she glanced at the

orchard as they passed by. No weeds or overgrowth of vines grew among the bare apple trees. In the farther end of the area, a row of pecan trees flourished. An occasional dried fruit, plum maybe, still clung to the branches of another clump of trees.

Madison dug her feet into the ground. "Ben, wh— what happened to the weeds and limbs that were here when we first walked this way?" Now, she was stuttering.

Ben turned to the man in the suit. "The woman is delirious. Perhaps a concussion. We need to call Dr. Dankworth as soon as possible."

The other man gripped her arm harder. "Madam, you must be careful."

If the man was so concerned about calling his doctor, why didn't he pull out his cell phone?

Madison had to admit she felt strange. Wouldn't hurt to talk to the doctor, but why didn't they take her to the acute care clinic in Travisburg?

Finally, they arrived at the Thatcher estate where they'd met with Ms. Maddox. The cedar shingles and fieldstone borders had somehow been restored to look like new. The porch had been given a fresh coat of paint and a set of wicker chairs sat on either side of a wooden table. Madison shook her head and blinked, sending a wave of nausea through her. How could they have accomplished this so quickly? Something wasn't right.

The wooden porch stairs were steeper than she expected, and Madison tripped on the first one. As if she was a sack of flour, Ben scooped her up and carried her onto to the porch. "I'd like to speak with Ms. Maddox, please." Maybe she could make sense of this.

The man in the baggie suit held the door while Ben

carried her in. "I'm sorry, ma'am, but I don't know of anyone by that name."

Instead, an attractive woman of around thirty rushed toward them. "Sir, can I be of assistance?" Her wide, chunky high heels clinked across the floor. In a two-piece outfit with a stripped jacket and fitted shirt, she appeared to be dressed for work. The tailored suit was nothing like the clothing Macys or Nordstroms sold.

"Yes, Ethel, please help Benjamin get this woman to one of the empty bedrooms. And Benjamin, after you put her down, call the doctor immediately."

Did Madison really want to allow this woman to help her? Her heart pounded a little harder. Maybe they were kidnapping her and would hold her for ransom. But why did Ben seem to be on their side? And why did he pretend he didn't know her? Madison fought the tears which burned her eyes. *Please, Lord, help me.*

Ben set her down on a chair next to the bed and hurried out as Ethel shut the door after him.

She grasped an old-fashioned brush from the side table. "Allow me to get some of that dirt and grass from your hair." She brushed Madison's curls with long, gentle strokes and then turned down the chenille bedspread, fluffing the pillows covered with matching cloth. The lady who must've worked at the estate helped Madison to the unusually high bed. "Sit on the side of the bed, my dear."

"Ethel, how long have you worked here? We arrived this morning and only met with Ms. Maddox."

Ethel patted her hand and gave her a sympathetic smile. "Why don't you try to rest. The doctor will be along shortly." She pulled off Madison's muddy, turquoise tennis shoes and laid them on the paisley carpet. "I must ask, though. Where did you purchase those shoes? I have some sneakers, but yours are much different than mine. Perhaps in Europe?" She pulled back the blanket and sheets and helped Madison under the covers.

Finally, they were communicating. "I got these at the supermall in Fairville."

"Hmm, I've been to Fairville many times but am not familiar with a supermall."

This woman was rather out of touch, as far as Madison was concerned. A knock on the door alerted her that the doctor might have arrived.

Ethel scurried to the door. "Yes, Dr. Dankworth. The lady is resting."

The doctor passed the sitting area on the other side of the room with two armchairs covered in a rich flowered print and set his bag on a side table. He lifted his stethoscope as he approached Madison. "What is your name, Miss?"

For a few seconds, her name refused to form on her lips. "I—I'm Madison Montgomery, a real-estate photographer. My partner, Ben Taylor is here, too. He's the one who called you."

Dr. Dankworth glanced at Ethel and shook his head, obviously not believing a word she said. He turned back to Madison and placed the chest piece on her back and chest. "Take a deep breath, please."

He cleared his throat. "All right." He looked at the cut to the side of her forehead. "I'll dress this wound, but the cut isn't deep, and stiches won't be required. Should heal up quickly."

The doctor opened his black bag and dabbed some kind of disinfectant on her forehead. Then he covered the area with a small bandage. "Just rest for a few days. My concern is the obvious confusion. You may have hit your head quite soundly. We'll keep an eye on you and allow your injury to heal."

"But I can't stay here for a few days. My boss is expecting us home tomorrow." She steepled her hands. "Please send Ben back in here."

Ethel lifted the blanket to cover Madison. "Relax, dear. I'll fetch you some clothes." She slipped quietly into the hall.

Madison glanced around the room she realized was much larger than she originally thought. Long ceiling-to-floor velvet curtains covered paned windows on one wall. A tilted mirror sat on the marble top of a dresser.

Muffled voices in the hall caught her attention. She crawled out of bed, battling the urge to throw up, and shuffled to the door. She pressed her ear to the wood.

"Must be some type of amnesia. I suggest you let her rest. Perhaps her memory will return"

"But doctor, we don't know who she is. I hope she's not wanted by the law or something terrible like that."

"She is dressed rather oddly. She said she was a photographer. Perhaps she works for some magazine or newspaper."

"Maybe that would explain those dreadful work clothes. And her hair, it hangs like a red mop."

"But if she is to be believed, I don't understand why she claims to work with Ben Taylor, your gardener."

"Benjamin Taylor, yes."

"I suggest you offer her a place to stay until we can find out more. She obviously isn't in her right mind."

Madison rubbed her forehead. Did she have amnesia? And why this awareness of another place and another time? Eyes heavy, Madison moved back to the plush bed and allowed the drowsy waves to flow over her. Maybe after a quick nap, life would return to normal. Right?

Chapter Thirteen

Madison rubbed her eyes and sat up in bed. The aroma of sweet apples roasting tickled her nose and made her stomach growl. The chef at the Heidelberg Inn must be preparing more of the delicious apple cake for dessert. She felt around for her cell phone. She needed to check with Ben to see what time he wanted to go to dinner.

The sound of voices outside her room alerted her. Who was in the hall at the B&B? Did Ben have someone with him?

She rubbed her eyes again and looked around.

Wait.

This room was nothing like her Heidelberg room. Her heart sank as she remembered. Ben and another man brought her here, and the doctor had patched up the wound on her forehead. She softly ran her fingers over her forehead. Ouch.

The nice woman named Ethel had gone to get her some clean clothes. Madison peered at the bottom of the bed. A beautiful yet unique navy wool dress with ruffled sleeves lay to one side.

Madison slowly arose from the bed, fighting nausea, and slipped on the vintage dress. Remarkable.

The old-fashioned outfit looked to be brand new. Then she glanced into the bathroom's gold, framed full length mirror. She ran the brush through her curls to remove the last bits of leaves still entangled in her hair. Her pale skin contrasted with the golden freckles. Her makeup—well, she'd have to go for the natural look. No mascara, eyeshadow, or lipstick.

In the expansive, luxurious bedroom, she relaxed in the stuffed sitting chair and listened for Ethel. Madison could do without the confusion inside her head. If ever disorientation had taken possession of her brain, today was the day. One thing though—she had to continue with her photography—her boss's assignment. Get shots of the decorations and festivities at the mansion. He'd expect nothing but her best effort.

She glanced around the room. No camera anywhere. She'd arrived at the mansion empty handed. But she had to have her camera to finish her work. Nothing to do now but to return to the springhouse and search for it.

Ethel marched into the room. "Ah, Madison. How was your bath?" Ethel laughed. "My dress looks better on you than it does me."

Madison lifted a brow. She didn't care for her look at all. If she could locate her jeans and hoodie, she'd be happy.

Ethel ran a hand through her soft dark waves with the part on one side of her head. Pearl earrings and necklace matched her gray and white lace dress. The woman looked ready to go to church or an elaborate party. "You must feel better. I'm so glad. I've been so worried about you."

If Madison had a sister, she'd want her to be like

Ethel. Kind, attentive, considerate. But Ethel wasn't her sister, right? Madison rubbed her brow. A fog of disorientation crept along the corners of her mind.

No.

She couldn't forget why she was here at the Vanderheim mansion.

Then a brilliant notion hit. She figured it out. Ethel's vintage look, the man in the baggy suit who seemed to be in charge and a doctor who still made house calls, all of these people were a part of the Memories of Christmas Ball Kendrick had spoken about. They were preparing for the event by wearing costumes and getting into character. "Your costume is lovely. Where did you find such outfits, vintage in style yet not damaged or worn out?"

Ethel shook her head. "I'm sure I don't know what you mean. I always wear the latest styles." She touched Madison's shoulder. "I'll return shortly. I believe you could use a cup of hot chamomile tea, dear. Your face is pale."

Madison laughed. "That's because I don't have on any makeup. But I would appreciate a cup to settle my nerves. I suppose I freaked out when I awoke and found Ben treating me like I was nuts."

Ethel's eyes widened. "You what? Like those shows in a circus? I don't understand."

The woman determined to stay in character but for how long? "I appreciate your kindness, Ethel, but could you please ask Ben to come to my room? I need to discuss our assignment and see if he found my camera."

Ethel opened her mouth in a wide O. "Now I know. You're the photographer we hired to take photos at the ball."

"What? No." Madison smiled at the woman. "You're doing a great job preparing for the Memories of Christmas Ball, but I'd appreciate it if you'd lose the character for a while."

Ethel slapped her hand over her mouth. "What? I could never abandon the moral qualities my mother taught me."

A knocked sounded at the door.

Ethel turned to answer.

Madison strained to hear the whispered words.

"Yes, sir. I'll be right there." Ethel stepped back into the room. "Excuse me, Madison. Robert needs me to take a letter. But first I'll fetch Benjamin for you."

Madison ran her fingers through her hair. The builder and owner of the mansion constructed in the 1930s was also named Robert. Very few people dictated letters today. In fact, hardly anyone sent letters out in the age of emails. These two characters were truly devoted to the Memories of Christmas project.

Madison relaxed into the chair and fought the temptation to close her eyes. No. If she'd had a concussion, that was the last thing she needed to do. She gingerly touched the bandage on her forehead. Several days to heal? No way. She was ready to return to her normal activities right away.

She tapped her foot on the soft patterned carpet and arose, opening the bedroom door. Where was Ben? Ethel said she'd send him. No problem. She'd find Ben on her own.

Her head swam and waves of nausea swept over her. She gulped and grabbed her stomach. She wasn't going anywhere right now.

Back in the chair, Madison closed her eyes this time, allowing the sick feeling to pass.

"You asked for me?"

At the sound of Ben's voice, she opened her eyes. Why did he sound so proper?

"Ethel said you sent for me. I can't imagine why you would care to speak to me. But how may I be of assistance, madam?"

Ben still wore his costume, but what in the world was he thinking? They had an assignment to do. They hadn't been invited to participate in a celebration or to photograph it.

She looked him up and down. "You're really into the spirit of the season. I like the look of your wig and those period clothes, but Ben, quit messing around. We've got work to do." She rose from her chair.

Ben lifted his eyebrows and widened his eyes. "Madison, I have endeavored to clean my shoes before entering the house. And I believe I informed you that my name is Benjamin." He pulled at his hair. "I can assure you this is not a wig. It's all mine."

Another dizzy wave unsteadied Madison. If she ever made it back to Fairville, she'd tell Ben what she thought about his behavior at Mrs. Thatcher's estate as well as report him to Kendrick and recommend he fires the weird guy. And what was with him calling her Madison? He usually referred to her as Maddie.

"Look, I know you're not feeling well. You took quite a fall." He grasped her elbow. "Please sit down."

Madison quieted herself a few moments and then

rested her head in her hands. "I did fall, but I can't imagine that the injury could affect me like this. One more question. What do you think Kendrick is going to say when he learns we're delayed and didn't finish our job taking pictures? Frankly, I'm afraid we might get fired."

Ben shook his head. "I'm sorry. I'm not as patient as Ethel. Who is Kendrick and what pictures are you talking about?"

"I'm not sure what kind of game you're playing, but if nothing else, can you please help me find my camera? My career depends on it. It must be somewhere on the ground around the springhouse."

"Yes, I'll have a look now. What kind of camera do you have?"

"You should know, Ben. It is the latest Nikon mirrorless."

Ben shook his head. "I've never heard of a camera by that name."

Chapter Fourteen

Madison sat up straight in the chair. Had she fallen asleep? Where was Ben, and did he find her camera?

She slowly arose and stepped to the window.

A light dusting of snow on the lawn glowed bright as the moon peeked through thin clouds. Flakes settled on the shrubs and smaller trees lining the walkway from the drive to the main road. Though the cloudy sky fought to hide the moon, light reflected on the jagged peaks surrounding the area.

How long had she slept. The clock on the fireplace mantel said seven-forty. Her stomach growled. Had she missed dinner?

Tap. Tap.

"Madison, it's Ethel."

Madison opened the door to the woman she'd discovered was Robert's secretary. Madison splayed her fingers on her chest. "You look amazing."

Ethel's red satin dress with matching belt fit her slender waist and hips and then flared with a flow of material to her calves. "Dinner is served. I hope you can join us in the dining room."

Madison peered down at her own wool dress Ethel

had loaned her. "This is all I have to wear. Is it okay?"

"Don't worry. Though we usually dress for dinner, everyone understands your circumstances." She stepped into the hall. "I'll find some more things for you later this evening. Now, follow me."

At the bottom of the wide staircase, Ethel walked to the right past the expansive living room into an equally large dining room.

Resisting the urge to let out a whistle, Madison viewed the room's paneled walls. "This room is likely the size of my entire apartment."

Ethel lifted her brow. "I'm sure you're mistaken about that." She smiled and pointed to the far end of the long, rectangular table set for five. "We can accommodate twenty-five guests when Robert wants to entertain."

"Will Robert sit at the head of the table?" Madison glanced toward the far end.

"Oh, yes. Dr. Dankworth is our guest tonight so he'll sit next to Robert, then you can sit in the next seat. I'll be across from the doctor."

Madison's gaze darted around the room. The formality of the dining ritual was nothing like she'd ever known.

Ethel sat to the left of Robert's chair. "Benjamin will be seated next to me."

"Ben, he'll be here?" She took her seat in front of a series of red candles each resting amid an evergreen base on the white tablecloth.

"He supervises the estate, the landscaping as well as Robert's gardens and greenhouses. But more importantly, he's like family to Robert."

If Madison didn't know better, she'd believe she

dined at Robert Vanderheim's table in the 1940s. She'd read that wealthy people enjoyed formal, multi-course meals in the evening. She sat back in the simple but finely carved wooden chair and blew out a breath. Might as well keep up with the pretense and have fun.

The sound of men's voices alerted Madison that the others had arrived. She nodded at the doctor who slipped down beside her.

Across the table, Ben spoke. "Good evening."

Good evening? She'd never heard him talk in such a formal manner. She couldn't wait to speak to him after dinner. Placing the white cloth napkin in her lap, she sipped cold water from the crystal glass.

An older woman in a black dress and frilly apron edged past the seven-foot fir. Twinkling white and gold lights rested on the soft branches underneath the wings of an antique angel. She placed a salad of mixed greens with pecans, dried cherries and blue cheese in front of each guest.

After Robert said a prayer, Ethel picked up her fork. "Our cook creates the loveliest up-to-date meals most nights. Tonight, we'll have chicken breast stuffed with sweet apples, sliced sweet potatoes, a vegetable medley, and assorted cookies which I prepared myself."

Madison glanced around at the people at the table—the actors playing Ethel, Robert, and Dr. Dankworth. "You're all doing a great job of preparing for the Memories of Christmas Ball. I'm sure Anabel will be pleased."

Robert frowned. "Anabel? Of whom do you speak?"

Madison penned him with a stare. "The one selling the estate." If these people were insistent on staying in character, they wouldn't know of her. "Never mind. I suppose I was confused." She shook her head and chewed a bite of salad. She had to remember to play along with these actors.

Robert dabbed his mouth with his napkin and turned to Dr. Dankworth. "Have you heard of the latest vehicle they're developing for the military? It's a light-weight reconnaissance car that has four-wheel drive for off-road use. I wish I could get my hands on one."

Dr. Dankworth nodded. "Yes, is that the Jeep? I've seen photos in the newspaper. Would be mighty useful on your property, Vanderheim."

Robert glanced at Ethel. "I know they're building them for the army. But maybe I could pull some strings to buy one. First thing tomorrow, look into that, will you."

Ethel's face turned a soft pink. "Yes, of course. I agree, the vehicle would work well out here on your property."

Ben finished the last of his salad and set his fork by his plate.

Madison chuckled under her breath. No doubt, he'd go along with the charade they played at the dining room table. "Hey, Ben. Seen any good movies lately?"

"No, but I'm looking forward to seeing *The Philadelphia Story* when it opens after Christmas. I love Katherine Hepburn. Golly, she was hilarious in *Bringing Up Baby*."

Madison squinted her eyes. "Really, Ben?"

Ethel laughed. "I saw the stage production of *The Philadelphia Story* in New York City last March. Such a clever story. And Cary Grant stars with her in the movie. He's a real dreamboat."

Though he likely thought no one was looking, Robert winked at Ethel. Was he flirting with her? Maybe they were married in real life. What did Madison expect of two actors playing the part of two people who had an obvious attraction?

A different kitchen helper served the main course and later picked up the plates. Finally, the cook herself arrived with a large tray of Christmas cookies and steaming carafes of coffee.

"Ah, thank you Betty." Robert poured cream in his coffee. "Delicious as usual."

"My pleasure, Sir."

This was no eat and run meal—each course savored before the next one arrived. Madison welcomed the coffee as her eyes grew heavy.

Ben rose from the table humming "You are my Sunshine," a song she remembered hearing her grandmother sing. "Excuse me. I need to tend to a couple of shovels I didn't get a chance to put away. The snow is coming down a bit harder, and I need to get them into the tool shed."

Madison crossed her arms in front her. Ben. She might know he'd avoid talking to her again. He'd been so evasive all day. Honestly, he wasn't the same Ben here at the mansion as he was back home. She still didn't know if he'd found her camera. "Hope to speak to you later."

He shrugged and continued out of the room.

Madison slipped on a coat she found hanging on a

coat tree near the front door. With shoulder pads, the wool garment hung below her knees halfway to her ankles and cinched at the waist. She didn't care what the coat looked like as long as it kept her warm on the front porch. The fresh air would do her good, perhaps clear her head.

A cold breeze gusted over the dark sky, stinging her cheeks. The wisp of wind sounded like a flute. In the faint moonlight, she saw a shadow of a person creep across the yard. Was he dangerous? Perhaps she should return to her room.

She peered closer. "Ben. What are you doing?"

Ben glanced up from whatever thoughts had captivated his attention and walked toward her.

"Why are you out there?" She asked a question again and sat on the first step leading from the porch to the front yard.

"As I told you earlier in the dining room, I'm returning this shovel to the tool shed. Work always comes first, you know." He propped the shovel against the side of the house and sat down beside her.

So unlike Ben—the Ben who took time to enjoy the trees though they needed to get to Travisburg for a tire repair and to check into their hotel.

As if attempting to look into her soul, he studied her face and peered at her eyes. "Madison, you intrigue me. I think you believe I'm another man you call Ben. I've told you a lot of times, no one calls me Ben except my mom."

An icy chill ran through her, as if he'd doused her with a bucket of slushy snow. How could this guy not be Ben? He had the face she knew as Ben Taylor—and the muscular body. "You, you look exactly like him," she whispered. "What am I to think?"

"Everyone has a twin somewhere."

She shook her head hard and gripped her cheeks. He made her nervous, made *her* stutter. But Ben didn't stutter now. "I don't know. I'm so confused."

"Madison, even though you're a stranger, Robert provided a place for you to recuperate after that fall you had. If you want my opinion, you need to rest. Go up to bed and maybe tomorrow you'll feel better."

For the first time in years, she wished Ben had called her Maddie like he used to. She rose to walk back into the house. "I forgot to ask. Did you find my camera?"

"No, I'm sorry." He shook his head. "I searched the area and found nothing."

Tears threatened to form in the corners of her eyes. Her prized possession. Gone.

What about her boss? Would he understand when she explained that she was stuck at the Vanderheim property? And how could she notify him? Her stomach roiled. Where was her purse with her cell phone and ID? She hadn't seen it since she arrived. The battery had probably died by now. She tapped her forehead. Why hadn't she thought sooner? Maybe tomorrow she could ask Ethel if she could borrow her cell phone or even the landline at the house.

As she returned to her room, the festive red and green garlands strung along the hallway walls lifted her spirit a bit. Tomorrow. That was it. Tomorrow everything would be back to normal.

Chapter Fifteen

The warmth of sunlight wrapped around Madison like the comfortable quilt on her bed at the inn. She turned to her side and nuzzled her face into the pillow. The fresh aroma of lavender soothed her fears from yesterday. Thankfully, she'd only dreamed about Ethel and Robert and the strange Benjamin. In moments, she'd meet her friend Ben Taylor for breakfast.

She sat up in bed and rubbed her eyes. Had she finished her job at the mansion? Taken all the shots? She inched her legs off the bed and circled her feet on the heavy carpet. Where were her slippers? She wiggled her toes into the pair by her bed.

Standing, she glanced around the expansive bedroom. Her room at the Heidelburg wasn't this big, was it? Out the window, she saw a wide lawn. Beyond were buildings she'd photographed only yesterday. As if Ben had slid a snowball down her back, a shiver raced along her spine and settled in her stomach with an icy plunge.

She wasn't at the local inn at Travisburg. She was still at the mansion where she'd fallen and hit her head. This couldn't be happening. Last night, she'd been sure

...

"I'm telling you, Ethel, either this young woman is a bad egg, or she isn't well. I think it best …"

Madison crept to the door and paused. A man spoke. Was it the property owner?

"Shh, sir. She may hear you."

A knock on the other side of the door sent Madison stepping backward toward the center of the room.

"Madison, it's Ethel. May I come in?"

"Y—yes." Was she still in bed dreaming, or was Ethel real? She opened the door to the lovely woman with dark hair combed in tight curls around her ears, the same woman she'd met last night. Or was it last night? "Good morning. Or at least I think it's morning."

A slight frown on her forehead and eyes wide, Ethel's expression seemed to communicate compassion. "Yes, dear, it's seven in the morning. I wanted to see how you're feeling and if you'll be ready to come to breakfast about eight. Mr. Vanderheim is, er, concerned about you."

Madison gripped her cheeks and searched the room around her. She must've had a terrible fall. Was she roaming around in an altered state of consciousness? Would she return to the Heidelburg soon?

Taking a few steps closer to the beautiful woman dressed in period costume, Madison touched her shoulder. Yes, she was real.

Madison sighed. She'd always been a rational person, able to solve her problems with reason and logic. Before she and Ben started out on the job, she'd learned that the estate was originally owned and operated by the man who'd built it. A late Mr. Robert Vanderheim. Chills raced down her spine. "Ethel, Mr.

Vanderheim is the owner of this property, correct?"

Ethel frowned. "Yes, dear." She smoothed the skirt of her long sleeved, green fitted dress with a green and gold belt.

Madison held her breath. "And his first name is Robert."

"That's correct."

Could he possibly be the same Robert Vanderheim she'd read about? As if treading water in a swimming pool, Madison swayed. She reached for the arm of the nearby chair and sank into it. That was out of the question.

Ethel rushed toward her. "Are you all right?"

"Does Robert have a father or grandfather named Robert?" Perhaps he was a relative of the original Robert Vanderheim who developed the property.

"No. I believe his father's name was Charles, and he's never mentioned his grandfather." Ethel placed the back of her hand on Madison's forehead. "Perhaps I should get you back in bed and bring your breakfast to you?"

Another chill raced through her. "Can you tell me? What is the year?"

Ethel shook her head and patted Madison's hand. "Why, dear, it's 1940."

Madison poked at her waffles covered in maple syrup. She downed the orange juice topped with mint and shoved the plate of creamed ham and mushrooms away. Though the food tasted delicious, her appetite had fled. What was she to do with Ethel's proclamation? This was the year 1940? If they were still acting, the charade had gone too far. Madison shivered again. Either Ethel spoke the truth, or Madison had lost her mind. Every indication pointed to the latter.

Pushing back from the table, Madison slid her chair in place. Find Ben. He'd have the answers and could steer her back to reality. She donned her coat from the rack near the door.

Outside, she walked onto the porch and down the stairs. She gripped her fists into tight balls. Surely, she'd find answers. And what about the assignment her boss had sent her to do? She had to finish the job.

Another chill ran down her back. If Ethel told the truth, and the year was 1940, her boss hadn't even been born yet. She slumped against the railing at the bottom of the stairs.

After a few minutes, she moved away from the house's entrance. She shuffled down a path of irregular flagstones curving around beds of colorful pansies and violas in freshly tilled soil. Larger flagstones created steps leading down the gentle hill.

The sound of men's voices drew her toward the gardens closer to the apple barn. Grateful for the sun and windless day, she unbuttoned her coat.

Benjamin, in stiff blue jean overalls with a tan cotton button up shirt, spoke with a group of workers as they stacked roughhewn stones forming a rock wall. He turned to the mound of rocks and selected one, handing it to the worker. Like a puzzle, they fit each piece together, without using mortar. He strode from one worker to the next inspecting their work, complimenting one and directing another to make small changes.

Would the stuttering Ben she'd known for years work in a similar manner, showing the leadership this Ben did? Confused once more, she stopped and grabbed onto the rough trunk of a leafless birch.

Ben glanced up. "Good morning. Did you sleep well?"

How could she when she'd become lost in another time? "Fine, thank you." She sauntered closer to him. "Benjamin, I really need to talk to you."

One of the workers called to Benjamin. "Mr. Taylor, how do you like the angle of the stones in this last section?"

"Yes, it has to be a gradual curve to follow the edge of the road. The wall will protect this garden from erosion—that's the most important consideration. The appearance isn't my concern."

Madison couldn't believe her ears. "But what about the aesthetics of the stone wall. In eighty years, you want people to still admire your work."

"I'm not going to be around in eighty years. Right now, I need to do a good job for Mr. Vanderheim. He wants a stone wall, and he'll get one." He smiled at her. "Madison, I can see you are an intelligent woman. I'm sure you might enjoy some of the activities Ethel and the other female servants are doing in preparation of the Memories of Christmas Ball." He patted her hand.

She caught her breath. Since high school, she'd never heard Ben talk like this. But then, Benjamin seemed very different than the guy who'd accompanied her on the assignment. "May I please speak to you for a moment in private?" How could he have changed so much in the last couple of days? Unless … unless he wasn't the Ben she knew.

Benjamin walked closer and gripped her elbow. "Let me help you to the garden chairs closer to the house. You look pale." He gently grasped her hand and steered her toward the house.

At the edge of the colorful garden, a stone bench sat under a small Norway Spruce. "Here you go." Benjamin slid down beside her and continued to hold her hand. His sympathetic tone carried a hint of condescension. "Now what is it you needed?"

She stared at him. She had no choice but to go along with his game—the Benjamin who sat with her and held her hand. "Did you look again for anything I might have dropped when I fell?"

He nodded. "I went back again earlier this morning. I did a thorough search of the area and found nothing. You said you lost your camera. A camera bag would be noticeably large and easy to spot. Not to mention your tripod."

Was he out of touch? Her camera was about the size of a small box of crackers. Besides, she didn't need a tripod for daytime photos. The bag could've slid anywhere under a rock or bush—unless—unless the camera she used hadn't been invented yet. She shivered. "Can you check one more time, and this time take me?"

He shrugged. "I'm not sure what good that will do, but I'll be happy to take you after lunch."

A few hours later, Madison followed Benjamin over

the sturdy, wooden bridge spanning the creek toward the springhouse. He carried a brown bag with him, but he didn't say what was in it.

At the edge of the woods, she spotted the area where his drone crashed. "Ben, er, Benjamin, have you thought about searching for your drone?" Would he play along with the charade or now that no one was around, would he answer her honestly? "I believe it landed right over there." She pointed toward the evergreen tree.

He glanced back at her and then waited for her to catch up along the path. His tone was soft and sympathetic. "You mentioned that earlier. Are you referring to a radio-controlled aircraft? I have heard of them but don't know why you would think I had one." He patted her shoulder. "It's not good for you to mention it again. People might think you're a spy. You'll get your bearings in a few moments. We're almost at the springhouse." He gripped her hand with his warm one, bringing a sense of security for a moment.

Was this her future? Living on this enormous property with this man named Benjamin, so different from another Ben she once knew?

No. She had dropped her camera bag. It must've landed somewhere in this area. She couldn't lose sight of the reality she'd once known.

Benjamin tugged her forward and glanced up the hill. "We're here—at the springhouse. Let me show you where I found you."

She widened her eyes as she gazed at the stone stairs leading to the top of the structure. Each stone looked as if the gardeners had built the walkway up the steep incline only last week. No sign of moss or dirt marred them.

Madison followed Benjamin up the narrow steps to the top level where the smaller stairs veered around to the left and farther up the hill.

"I found you here, on the step level with the opening to the springhouse. You lay unconscious." He bent toward her, as if examining her forehead.

She picked up the aroma of fresh dirt and evergreen trees. Not an unpleasant scent, but manly.

"Looks like your wound is healing. I'm so glad. I was sincerely worried about you."

"Thank you, but I can't wait to ask. What is this structure used for?"

"In the past, most of these small buildings were used for storage of dairy products and other perishables. Mr. Vanderheim constructed this as an addition to his garden. In the future, he could use it for refrigeration but for now, it's a part of his water features."

The arch-shaped structure protruded from the side of the hill. Madison poked her head into the rectangular door in front.

Benjamin stood behind her so close she could feel his breath on her neck. The warmth from his body sent a tingle down her spine.

"The cool spring water emerges from underground here at the back of the springhouse. It falls into this small pool and runs out through an underground conduit."

He gripped her elbow when she stepped out of the house. "Careful." He held onto her until they reached the edge of the hill.

Madison rested her hand on his shoulder to steady

herself. "What's that?" She pointed up to a miniature set of stairs leading to a doll sized castle nestled between the roof of the springhouse and the upper platform.

"Oh, I asked Robert about that. He said one of the workers built it. Some foolishness about a home for the fairies. I guess the worker's daughter must come here to play."

"I don't think it's foolishness. I find it a delightful sentiment." Below, water rushed from the opening of the pipe in the springhouse and flowed into a small waterway down the side of the hill. She glanced around the area where he'd indicated he'd found her. "You said I fell and landed on this platform. My camera must've come to rest somewhere around here." If she could only find it, she could prove to herself—and the rest—that she hadn't gone crazy.

A dizzy spell threatened. She grasped a rock in an effort not to roll down the hill.

Benjamin wrapped his arms around her and guided her to the steps just below where she'd awakened. Maybe if she remained quiet a moment, things would return to normal, and she'd find the Ben she'd always known. She leaned against him and closed her eyes.

How many moments later, she wasn't sure. She opened her eyes.

Ben or Benjamin smiled at her with a small paper bag in his hand. "Madison, I brought us a snack for our walk. Perhaps you'll feel better if you eat something."

Still wearing his overalls, Ben opened the bag he'd been carrying and unwrapped a wax paper package and passed the bundle with crackers and cheese to her. "I'm quite concerned about you. I have some chocolate candy bars if you'd like one."

The cheddar cheese and crispy crackers tasted delicious and seemed to clear her head. She took a bite of the rich, creamy chocolate.

"Better?" Benjamin gripped her hand and then glanced around toward the gardens. "I need to get back to my work, but let's take another quick look for that camera of yours. You said your camera was in a bag. About what size is it?"

"About this big." Madison held up her hands to demonstrate the camera bag's dimensions.

Benjamin frowned. "I'm sorry, Madison, but I can't imagine any camera bag that small which would accommodate all your equipment, not to mention film cartridges."

Chapter Sixteen

Madison pressed her hand against her stomach and collapsed into the wicker chair on the porch. She exhaled a heavy sigh. Her one hope of connecting to the world she'd always known had flittered away. Her equipment—perhaps a figment of her imagination—never to be found.

She gazed at the snow-covered mountains in the distance. She had to admit that the Vanderheim mansion was situated in a stunning area between two mountains dotted with evergreen trees. Life here wouldn't be that bad.

Noise inside the mansion sparked her curiosity. Something was up. Madison rose and strolled inside through the wide double doors at the front entrance.

One of the servants rushed by, her arms filled with an open box of what looked like Christmas decorations. Colorful balls, holly, bows, and red candles.

"Madison, you're just in time." Ethel sauntered toward her in three-inch brown leather shoes which clacked along the hardwood floor. "The Christmas Ball is in one week on Christmas Eve." She laughed. "I fear it will take that long to get this home decorated."

Madison giggled under her breath. If she couldn't

work on her photography assignment, she might as well decorate a mansion in the year 1940. "Of course. Let me know what to do."

"Follow me." Ethel nodded and led her to a room off the main entry.

She gasped when she entered the expansive room. Would she ever lounge in one of the upholstered dark red chairs along the perimeter of the cherry paneled walls? She walked across the polished floor which lay empty, ready for dancers to celebrate. Tall antique glass windows on the other side afforded a view of the forest below.

Ethel pointed to one end with three stained glass windows each with nautical scenes in shades of blue and green. "The musicians will perform from over there. They play Appalachian music like many people in the area enjoy."

"So, who's invited to this ball?"

Ethel's smile filled her face, and she clasped her hands. "We invite everyone in the area. The hard-working farmers from the settlement just west of us, the town's people, anyone who wants to celebrate with their neighbors and friends. We've held the ball for several years now. I believe Robert intends to continue for as long as the good Lord allows."

As if they'd summoned him, Robert called to Ethel from outside the room before stepping into the doorway.

Ethel brushed her fingers against her chest. "Excuse me." She sauntered to the other side of the room stopping only a few feet in front of him. She glanced at her feet and then up to Robert.

Madison couldn't disguise the grin. If she didn't

know better, she'd believe Ethel was in love with the owner of the mansion.

After dinner, Madison returned to the ballroom with Ethel and floated from one tree to the next. "The sparkling lights glistening on the decorated trees lining each wall transforms the room into a winter wonderland." She giggled. "Like fireflies flitting around the room." She spied an ornament which had fallen off one of the trees. Picking up the breakable object, Madison hooked the silver hand-painted ornament with the red poinsettias on the tree once more.

Ethel steepled her hands. "You have such an imagination. Thank you for the complement. We still have much more to do. Like decorating the banisters on the staircase to the second floor."

Madison glanced toward the ceiling and the strings of silver garland strung from one wall to the chandelier in the middle of the room and then to the opposite wall. "I wish I could snap a few shots."

"Oh, don't worry. We've hired a photographer especially for that night. He will take photographs of the room and the food table in the dining room. But he also takes shots of the families and dating couples." Ethel paused, staring at the red shiny bright ornaments on the tree across the hall from her.

Finding the courage to ask, Madison walked closer and smiled. "Please forgive me if this is none of my business, but I think you see Robert as more than a boss. Am I right?"

Ethel's mouth dropped open. "Oh, no, Madison. He's my employer and nothing more. Besides, there's a big age difference between us. I'm thirty and he's forty-two."

Clasping Ethel's hands in hers, Madison gave a soft chuckle. "I can't imagine that would make any difference. If you two are in love … " The thought of this unlikely romance struck a happy chord inside. "I think he likes you. The way he looks at you … Can't you tell?"

Ethel led Madison out of the room and into the hall. "Let's talk here. I'd rather the servants not hear us." She stared out the window a moment and then caught Madison's gaze. "All right. I'll admit. I have been in love with him since the first month of my employment. But I couldn't possibly tell him. It would be too presumptuous."

Madison glanced down at the thick Sears catalogue sitting on a side table. "Maybe you don't have to tell him but allow him to make the first move."

"How?" Ethel lifted her brows.

Madison thumbed through the catalogue. "You are a very beautiful woman. Perhaps with a little more blush on your cheeks and—" She flipped the pages. "Here." She pointed to a dress featured in the spring and summer section. "See. The top is fitted and the flowery material gathers at the waist. Then the skirt flares, displaying your hourglass figure." She winked at Ethel. "You'd look lovely in that."

"But do you think Robert is too old to be interested in romance?"

Madison threw back her head and laughed. "Are you kidding? Not when a radiant woman like you is there to intrigue him."

Ethel dropped into the chair near the side table and began flipping the pages. "Hmm. I think I'll order that one."

"Good idea."

Ethel looked at the catalogue a few more moments and then up to Madison. "There's something I've wanted to ask you if I may."

"Yes?"

"I'd like to know more about you. Where do you come from."

Madison had expected the question sooner or later. But she couldn't tell her she came from a time eighty years in the future. "I'm from Fairville, about three hours from here if you drive."

"And what brought you to our area?"

"I'm a photographer."

But again, she had to withhold the fact that the Vanderheim property was up for sale. "I, er, can't really get into the entire story."

Chapter Seventeen

Ping. Ping.

Something tapped on the window. Consciousness returned and Madison opened her eyes. Where was she? She'd gone to sleep in her comfortable bed at the Vanderheim estate last night. What made the noise, and was she back to the life she'd always known?

She turned her head to look up at the pale blue hand-painted ceiling with clouds adorning the space. In each corner, birds appeared to flap their wings as if in flight.

She sat up, gripping the pillow to her chest, and glanced toward the window.

Rain. Streams of water trickled down the panes in the Vanderheim bedroom. So, she hadn't returned to Travisburg or Fairville, and would she ever?

Finding the house shoes Ethel had loaned her, she stood and walked to the chair under the window to get a better view of the outdoors. No dizzy waves washed over her. If nothing else, she felt fine. Three days at the estate might've done her good.

A thought dawned. What did her boss think? She obviously wasn't answering her cell phone, which she'd stashed in her camera bag, and she didn't know where they had landed. Was Mom worried? The concern faded—perhaps as fast as the thought had arrived. Her fears no longer mattered.

She shook her head, splashed a little water on her face, and donned the outfit Ethel had loaned her. Baggie wool pants and a plaid button up, long sleeved coat. Her main goal now was helping Ethel with the decorations for the ball and … she snickered, playing matchmaker between Ethel and Robert.

After breakfast, she returned to the ballroom to place the blue and silver mercury glass ornaments on the last tree.

Ethel hauled in a box and set it on the floor. "Here's a few more things to put on this tree for the finishing touches, some strands of tinsel and snowflake paper cutouts. The snowflakes were made by some of the Cooks Cove children a few years back."

Madison smiled. "I really enjoy decorating. In my past, I've always seemed to be in a hurry. It's nice to slow down and appreciate what I'm doing." Somewhere on the other side of the room, "White Christmas" played on a radio.

Ethel clasped her hands on her waist and looked toward the end of the room. "We need one more tree for the entry next to the stairs. Would you like to go with Benjamin when he cuts one down? Might be a fun experience."

"Okay. I'd like that." But would Benjamin want her to go?

Madison slipped on Ethel's warm jacket and sauntered closer to the door.

Benjamin rushed in, a frown on his face. He looked around the room and then his gaze fell on her. "Are you ready? I've been waiting outside."

Picking up her pace, Madison grabbed the scarf off the hat rack and swirled it around her neck. "I'm sorry. Ethel only mentioned going with you a short while ago. You look like you're in a hurry." She snickered. Like she always had been before …

He stared at her. "Madison, I work as efficiently as possible. Mr. Vanderheim expects the best from me."

Pleasing Robert Vanderheim seemed to be a big deal for him. Well, she couldn't blame him. She wanted to do the best by Kendrick Grayson. Just not in such a fierce, rapid pace—she'd begun to realize.

At the tool shed, Benjamin selected what looked like a well-used ax with a steel head and wooden handle. "All right. Let's go."

A yellow lab rounded the corner and gave a sharp, friendly bark.

"Whose dog is that?"

"He belongs to Mr. Vanderheim. Sam enjoys following me sometimes."

Madison reached to pet his head.

"Oh, don't do that. He may not like you. You need to get acquainted first."

"Okay." No doubt he knew the dog's habits. Too bad, as she loved dogs. She'd ask Ethel about the pup later.

She followed Benjamin with Sam by his side across the bridge in the direction of the springhouse and to the woods beyond. "What size tree are you looking for?"

"Don't worry your pretty little head about that. I'll know it when I see it." He patted her hand. "Hopefully I can get one about twelve feet tall."

Madison picked up her stride to catch up with his fast ones. Though living in the 1940's held fewer demands, she felt more respected from men in her own time. Too bad she couldn't have the advantages of both time periods. Hmm. Maybe she could.

After a ten-minute hike into the woods, Benjamin lifted his hand. "Whoa. I think I've found the tree." He stopped in front of a gorgeous spruce. "A pine tree."

Madison tightened the scarf around her neck. "I believe it's a spruce with that thin scaly bark."

He squinted and curled his lips inward. "Look. I know my trees." He stepped a little closer. "Yes, as I said. This is a spruce."

Madison rolled her eyes. That's what she'd said in the first place, but it wasn't worth arguing over.

His face softened, and he circled his arm around her waist, leading her to a fallen log about twenty feet away. "I don't want anything to happen to you. That bump on your forehead was enough. If you'll sit here out of the way, you'll be safe."

Madison opened her mouth to protest. She wasn't an invalid. Maybe she could've helped. Well, if he insisted, she'd sit back and watch.

Sam ran up to her, probably glad he could see her at eye level. He sat on his haunches and lifted his paw.

"Awe, you want to shake hands." She smiled and shook his paw. Not the ferocious animal Benjamin had feared.

Sam gave her a quick kiss and ran back to Benjamin as if he wanted to assist.

Benjamin whacked the lower trunk of the tree, his muscled arms protruding under his heavy sweater. No doubt the Benjamin of the past was strong and capable. He looked every bit as handsome as the Ben she knew, but there was one difference. Benjamin didn't have the sweet, kind nature she saw in Ben.

"Okay, job done." Benjamin grasped the tree's trunk and drug the heavy load along the path.

"Can I help?"

He pulled her to his chest with his other hand. "Mr. Vanderheim and Ethel would never forgive me if anything happened to you. But you can carry the ax if you'd like."

That was it? He was concerned with what would happen to him and not her. She whistled for Sam who lobbed toward her from behind a tree. "Let's go, boy. Benjamin has a Christmas tree to haul back to the house."

Madison smiled at Benjamin as he held the chair for her to sit at the dinner table. From her spot, she had an easy view of the tree he'd cut down which the servants had already decorated with balls and lights.

Benjamin moved to sit across the table from her and gave her a flirty look.

Was he interested in her? Though she hadn't dated a lot in college, she could read his expression. Something like the way Robert looked at Ethel. Her face warmed, and she turned to Robert's secretary across from her.

Robert, at the head of the table, asked a blessing on

the food and then glanced up. "I requested my favorite soup for tonight. German noodle and butterball."

"Yes, it's spicy but creamy. The cook uses heavy cream and butter." Ethel smiled at Robert, and his return smile said what Madison had suspected. He was totally in love with her.

Benjamin took a sip of the soup. "Tell me, Madison. Do you like to cook? I would imagine you would."

What was she to say? *No, I have a full-time job as a photographer with a real-estate company. I eat fast food most of the time.* She cleared her throat. He'd believe she'd completely lost her mind if she said she ate at Taco Bell or Burger King. "Well, you see, I'm not much of a cook."

He widened his eyes. "What, a woman who doesn't cook? But then you make up for it in looks." He laughed.

If she wasn't a guest in the Vanderheim home, she'd tell the jerk what she thought of his remark.

Ethel must've noticed Madison's irritation. "What do you fancy doing in your free time?"

Most likely, they wouldn't understand a woman who goes rock climbing. "I enjoy hiking and exploring nature."

"Sounds lovely. Would you care to go to church with us tomorrow?"

"Yes, very much so."

Ethel stared at Benjamin. "What about you? Will you be joining us for the service. We're having a cookout afterward."

Benjamin shrugged. "No. Sunday is the only day I can work on my stamp collection. But I'll be there for the meal. A man has got to eat, you know."

Chapter Eighteen

The breakfast of poached eggs, biscuits, and smoked bacon settled in Madison's stomach. She pushed away from the table leaving her plate, silverware, and cups. Someone to clean up after her—a luxury she didn't have in Fairville.

"Robert will pull the car around front in a few minutes." Ethel placed her napkin on the table and stood.

"Let me grab my coat." Madison walked from the dining room to the large entry with the circular staircase.

Ethel followed and paced toward the stairs. "I'll get you one of my hats. Would you like a beret or a tilt hat?" Ethel offered.

Madison couldn't tell the woman she didn't know the difference much less that she never wore hats to church. "You choose, please. Whatever you think goes with my outfit." She glanced in the hall mirror at her clothing Ethel had laid out for her earlier. A purple and white patterned top with flared sleeves and matching pencil skirt.

"All right. I'll get you a pair of gloves as well. You know, the short ones that cover your hands to the wrist." Ethel hurried up the stairs.

Still gazing in the mirror, Madison shook her head. How styles had changed from Ethel's time to hers. She swallowed. Or would Ethel's time become her time? Life in Fairville seemed to fade more every day. Parkhill Christian Church seemed to dwell only in her imagination. She sank down onto the couch on the side of the stairs.

A broken piece of wood protruded from the wooden leg closest to the banister. Hmm. *How had this happened?*

Ethel returned with a purple hat shaped like a bowl. The two feathers with long shafts attached to the top—like no other Madison had seen.

"Hope this will do." Ethel handed the hat to Madison.

"Oh, yes. Thanks." Madison moved to the mirror, positioned the hat on her head, and then glanced toward the broken piece of wood on the couch's leg. "Did you see that nick in the sofa leg?"

Ethel laughed. "Sam chewed it when he was a puppy." She rushed out the front door with the dog close at her heels. "Sam, stay."

Robert, in the driver's seat of the coal-black sedan with *Chevrolet* written on the front, waited in front of the house.

Madison crawled into the second row. The red upholstered seats appeared brand new. She sniffed. The interior had that *new car* smell. She chuckled to herself. She would've deemed the vehicle an antique, but if the time was actually 1940, the car would be the latest model. Robert Vanderheim maneuvered the car, shoulders back and chin up. No doubt proud of his vehicle.

Ethel, sitting next to Madison, glanced toward the window and rolled the nob, bringing down the glass. "I love the fresh forest air."

Madison had to admit, she felt as if she acted in a movie. Soon the cameras would shut down, and the actors would return home. The life she'd always known would reappear. "Do you attend church in Travisburg?"

Ethel shook her head. "No, we worship at a small church in an area that used to be called Cook's Cove. Many of the local farming families attend."

"All right, ladies. We're here." Robert parked the car and opened Ethel's door to help her out and then extended his hand to Madison. "You may not know, but this church was built in one hundred fifteen days by a local resident with a hundred and fifteen dollars in his pocket. He wound up being the first pastor, as well."

Madison adjusted her sideways hat. "The man offered a great service to Cook's Cove."

Inside, they strolled down a long aisle past rows of wooden pews. An elderly woman plunked out "How Great Thou Art" on an out-of-tune piano in the front. Madison lifted her gaze to a wide window displaying the snow-covered mountains in the distance and the small graveyard dotted with markers. Though she felt like a foreigner in this area of Tennessee—and in this time period, one thing was true. God transcended all time. Even if she remained here at a time well before her mother gave her birth, the Lord was still with her.

Madison floated through the doors of the mansion and into the large entry. She turned to Ethel behind her. "Thank you for taking me to church today. Amazing how time with the Lord can help to lift heavy burdens."

"You're more than welcome." Ethel removed her wrap and hung her coat on the coat stand beside the door. "I'm sorry but your clothes you arrived in are still in the laundry. The rain prevented them from drying. But don't worry. I have some more things you can wear. I hung some additional dresses in your closet."

"Thank you. I'll go change now." She glanced at herself as she passed the hall mirror. "This beautiful outfit certainly wouldn't be appropriate for a cookout." Madison ran her hand along the smooth curved banister as she climbed the carpeted stairs. Wearing Ethel's outfit wouldn't stand out so much as if she wore her jeans. She increased her pace up the stairs. No time to waste as Ethel needed help with the preparations.

"Madison."

She jumped and turned as Benjamin climbed the stairs behind her, his long strides bringing him to her side as she arrived on the second floor.

"I'm glad I caught you. I wanted to discuss something with you." Ben led her to an alcove. "Sit for a moment."

She eased onto the blue velvet windowsill cushions, Benjamin beside her. The tall bay windows looked out onto the backyard stretching into the forest.

Her heart picked up speed. What did he want to talk about? Usually, she had to chase him down to have a few words.

He swallowed hard several times. Odd, he seemed nervous.

"Madison, I want you to know that Robert has spoken with me. He's troubled. On the day you arrived, there were no extra cars in the area. We don't know how you arrived, nor who you are. You say you are a photographer, which is unusual."

She sat and leaned against the side wall of the alcove, her back as stiff as a tree branch. "I don't understand."

Benjamin moved forward, his voice low. "With the war in Europe, people are cautious. Is it possible that you work for a foreign entity?" The muscles in Benjamin's jaw moved up and down as they tightened. His eyes, hard, fixed her with a stare.

Absurd. Her muscles tightened until she felt like an overfilled water balloon ready to burst. She couldn't restrain the waves of laughter which shook her as she stared at him.

"This is serious, Madison. They may ask you to leave. Or worse, call the authorities."

Gulping to control the outburst, Madison clasped her hands together. "I'm sorry, Benjamin. But that was far from what I expected. You can tell Mr. Vanderheim that I'm not a spy. And if I were, I no longer have memory of a mission or purpose at the mansion. Therefore, I'm useless to any foreign entity." Madison struggled to control the smile that tugged at her cheeks.

Whether he was convinced or not, she didn't know.

He rose from his seat as he continued to stare at her.

Did he think if he stared hard enough, he would read her thoughts?

Benjamin opened his mouth, then shut it again. Turning, he mumbled, "See you at the cookout."

Madison warmed her hands over the burning logs. The outdoor grill reminded her of the charcoal one her father used except Robert had constructed his to be a permanent fixture. The fire pit nestled between two sections of clean, white brick in front of a pyramid-shaped backdrop meant to keep sparks from flying into the forest behind.

"Excuse me, ma'am." A young man wearing a white apron neared the fireplace. He had what appeared to be a damp cloth protruding from his back pocket. He took it, wiped his hands, and tucked it back.

Clever.

Madison took a few steps to the right. "Sorry."

Using a long fork, the guy she assumed was one of the waiters, spread pieces of chicken out over a metal grate.

Madison crossed the stone surface to a large wooden picnic table covered with a red and white checkered tablecloth. She unbuttoned her heavy jacket and glanced at Ethel who sat in an outdoor chair. "This was a perfect day to have a winter picnic."

Ethel, huddled next to Robert, grinned. "We're fortunate to have these mild, December days.

Someone approached, his sudden nearness causing her to jump. She turned to her left.

Benjamin nodded toward Ethel and Robert and then nudged her farther to the side of the patio. "If I'm not mistaken, I believe they're keen on each other. What do you think?" He gazed at her with deep brown eyes, minus his usual twinkle. Clean shaven today, he looked so different from the Ben who operated drones and wore a five o'clock shadow most days.

Madison couldn't help but giggle. "I believe you're right." She wouldn't mention she'd already discussed the matter with Ethel.

After a half hour, the aroma of roasting meat made her mouth water.

Two other servants brought bowls of potato salad and cooked carrots, baskets of bread, molasses cookies, and carrot cake and set them in the middle of the table.

"The chicken should be ready to serve momentarily," the guy wearing the apron announced.

Ethel rose from her chair and walked closer to the grill.

Madison patted Benjamin's arm. "Excuse me. I'm going to see if I can help her."

Ethel faced the cook and then glanced at the coals. "Thank you, Jason. One more brush with the sauce and I believe it's ready."

The moist sauce hit the wood below and flared. A spark lifted out of the fire and landed on the edge of Ethel's skirt.

The fabric lit easily, the flame spreading upward in the blink of an eye.

Ethel screamed and started to run.

"No." Robert raced to them, brushing Madison aside. He grasped Ethel's arm. "Don't move."

Ethel tugged away from him. "I'm on fire."

Robert shook the boy's cloth free and slapped at the material.

With each brush, the fire died until it went out.

Madison drew nearer to her. "Did you get burned?"

Ethel brushed a tear from her face. "N—no, I don't

believe so."

Robert leaned toward her and grasped her elbow. "I'm so sorry, Ethel. I wish I could've protected you from the fire."

Madison's assumptions were confirmed. He cared for her.

Ethel threw her arms around him. "Thank you. I don't know what I would've done if you hadn't acted quickly."

He guided her to the chair again and inspected the material. "You might want to go change."

"I'll go with you." Madison stood to follow her.

The haunting sound of a flute emanated from somewhere in the woods. "Do you hear that?"

Benjamin shrugged. "Hear what?"

"I don't hear anything," Ethel said.

"I do." The boy, Jason, set the serving fork on the meat platter and wiped his hands on his apron. "Sounds like someone is in the forest playing a flute."

Chapter Nineteen

The next day, Madison paced the floor in the ballroom. She had to applaud Ethel and the servants. They'd transformed the room into a winter wonderland from the hanging garland to the brilliantly decorated trees to the polished floor.

But as beautiful as the décor was, nothing cheered her. She heaved a heavy sigh. Would her dismal mood lift, or had she better get used to her current frame of mind?

She glanced out the front window of the room.

Benjamin held a hose at the base of a small tree.

That was it. Instead of feeling sorry for herself, missing the old Ben, as well as her family, she needed to think of others. Help Benjamin with the gardening.

Madison slipped on Ethel's jacket over her two-piece, linen top and skirt and stepped outside on the front porch.

About twenty feet from the steps, Benjamin glanced up as she neared.

"That's a lovely tree you're watering."

He set the hose down and walked toward her. "Yes, I planted it in October along with a second one on the other side of the path. You're likely not familiar with the species." He gave her a shy-looking smile. "Species means a group of the same kind."

Madison's stomach tensed. Did he believe her to be uneducated. "I took a botany—"

"Most women leave tree planting to the men, anyway." He patted her hand. "This is a Japanese Maple."

"Japanese Maple?" She almost told him she had one at her apartment but clamped her mouth shut. No sense in opening up the topic of where she lived. He'd never believe her.

"Yes, Madison. They are beautiful in the summer with their purple-red leaves." He dug around the base of the little tree to loosen weeds and grass. "This Japanese Maple will get to around forty or more feet someday. Look, I think a walk around the property would do you some good." He glanced toward the orchard. "Shall we?"

"I suppose you're right."

After turning off the water, Benjamin led her through the fallen, dead leaves from last autumn and hard packed soil with twigs and withered grass to the rows of leafless apple trees.

She might as well get to know Benjamin better. "Do you plan to make this job your career?"

Benjamin stared at her as if he didn't understand the question. "The job working for Mr. Vanderheim? I haven't really thought about it." He ran his finger down the trunk of one of the trees.

Madison frowned. Odd. She would've thought he'd had his life figured out by now.

He reached for her shoulders and gently turned her to face him. "I understand you're a photographer." He gave her an easy smile. "In my opinion, women would be happier in the home. You know, doing all those things for her family. Preparing meals. Keeping the house clean. You could even take pictures to place them in a scrapbook or other mementos that women keep."

"What? You can't be serious?" Maybe the time period had something to do with these odd statements. But then, there had been many famous female photographers in the 1940's. She didn't care for his attitude at all. If she remained in 1940, she'd avoid a deeper relationship with him—though she had to admit to an attraction to this guy who reminded her of Ben.

"Shall we turn back?" Benjamin pinched his lips in a scowl. Apparently, he didn't care for her words, either.

Returning to the mansion right now felt to her as if she headed to jail. "I believe I'll continue on for a while. I can't get enough of this mountain air."

With a look that said he was concerned about her, he touched her shoulder and lowered his voice to a whisper. "Are you sure you'll be okay?"

She lifted her chin. "Of course. What could happen to me out here on the Vanderheim property?" Madison didn't look back to see his expression. She walked past the orchard and crossed the bridge over the little creek.

Rock climbing. If only she were with her friends on a climb today. Not that she had her equipment here, but she could look for an easy hike toward the mountain.

She gripped the thin, shedding bark on the trunk of a sycamore and rested her forehead on the tree. Face it. She was a foreigner in a strange place. And she'd likely always be.

Climbing was no fun without her friends, and her

friends were very far away. She batted at the tear on her cheek. Would she ever return to the life she'd always known, especially in time to celebrate Christmas with people she loved? With Ben?

The trill of a Winter Wren reminded Madison she lingered in the forest on the Vanderheim property. The thought of returning to the mansion to watch Ben performing his duties as a gardener tightened her chest and sent a wave of nausea to her throat. She couldn't go back now. Just a few more moments here in the forest where she belonged and everything seemed familiar, away from the confusion, the uncertainty of life in Benjamin's world.

She trekked on through the uneven terrain, stepping over exposed roots and avoiding small holes created by a burrowing creature.

The sound of rushing water drew her past an eight-foot-wide creek on her left. White, smoky sprays twirled and rushed down the river rocks. Traveling farther, a narrow, dirt road materialized ahead.

She continued along the edge of the road and then tapped her head. She'd been down this way before. Only yesterday when she attended church with Robert and Ethel. Another half mile, and she'd arrive at the place of worship.

Madison picked up speed. The memory of the roughhewn log building beckoned, the place where she'd sensed God's presence. "Lord," she whispered, "no matter what happens, You're here with me."

A moment later, the sun's rays filtered through the clouds reaching out like fingers to the little building. Madison gazed at the front of the church. Instead of going in, she veered to the right.

A small graveyard, perhaps where congregational members were buried, occupied the grassy hill beside the church. As if in reverence, Madison lightened her steps to walk with less noise.

She strolled along the first row and stopped at a weatherworn gravestone with an arched top. Walking closer, she read the faded inscription.

Martha A. Vanderheim

Born May 5, 1835

Died September 9, 1905.

Who knew? Perhaps she was one of Robert's relatives. Madison read the verse beneath. "From everlasting to everlasting, thou art God." Truth seeped into her heart, filling her with a sense of peace.

Madison rounded the graveyard returning to the front of the little church. She climbed the steps and tried the door. Open. Her footsteps echoed in the empty building as she made her way to the front. What was that verse on the tombstone? Psalm 90. Spotting the pulpit Bible, Madison opened it to the middle. Continuing where the stone left off, "Thou turnest man to destruction; and sayest, return, ye children of men. For a thousand years in thy sight are but as yesterday when it is past, and as a watch in the night." Madison's pulse settled into a steady, calm beat. God would take care of all generations who'd allow Him to. He was God in 1940, and He's still the God of her time. God was over all time. "Lord, thank You for showing me Your truth."

Madison had lived on earth only a short time, but if she had to admit it, she'd been downright cruel to Ben when they were younger, and probably to others as well. Her friends had always said mean things about others they thought less than them.

Madison bowed her head. All the time that they'd made their comments, she'd known that for some reason, they'd allowed her to be a part of their group, yet she considered herself less than them.

To feed her own sense of security and self-esteem, she'd stayed quiet. "I'm sorry. Please forgive me," she whispered to the Lord. "I don't want my life to continue here in Robert Vanderheim's time and never have a chance to ask for Ben's forgiveness. Please allow me to return home to Fairville—and Ben." Her kind and patient friend—the man she'd begun to realize she loved. Only the birds, forest creatures, and God heard her whispered words.

Chapter Twenty

Madison couldn't remain in the forest crying all day. The sunny winter morning battled the dark clouds that threatened to mimic her tears. She picked up her pace when the first few drops fell. She trekked on, her gaze toward the mountain that rose beyond the Vanderheim mansion. The leaves that had crunched and crackled under her feet now pinged as fat raindrops landed.

By the time the mansion materialized, the rain came down in sheets. Hoping she hadn't ruined Ethel's clothes, Madison stepped onto the porch. Water dripped from her like a saturated sponge.

A maid peeked through the door. "Stay put, Miss, until I get you a towel."

"Thank you."

Later after Madison dried off, she climbed the stairs to her room. The sooner she could get a warm bath, the better.

She slid deeper into the bathtub as the steaming water soothed her chilled body. "God, thank You for washing me, inside and out." Although her future was unsure, she was sure of God's forgiveness.

Madison's stomach grumbled, protesting the

skipped lunch. What would she wear, now that she'd soaked Ethel's outfit? Stepping from the bathroom, she spotted her jeans and hoodie folded neatly on the side table. "My clothes I wore when I arrived here." She couldn't help the grin. Slipping on the familiar outfit, she headed downstairs to find a meal.

"Madison, you poor thing." Ethel rushed toward her. "Winter in the mountains is like a treacherous woman. It can change from one moment to the next. Let's get you something to eat."

The sun headed toward the horizon. Madison wandered from one room to the next. After she'd explored the house, chatted with the maids, and pet the dog, she headed to the porch. Sitting on the first step, she glanced at the sky. Storm clouds moved across the heavens and disappeared as fast as they had come. She pulled in a long breath of wet grass and leaves.

The thin whistle of a sparrow reverberated through the trees. The fluttering of wings told her it had found a juicy worm crawling from the wet ground. Another bird sang a melody. Was it a wood thrush? She stood and stared in the direction of the music. No bird, but the graceful, silvery sound of a flute. She stepped off the porch and paced toward the sound. The mellow, ethereal melody wafted even louder through the pines as she tramped in the direction of the forest once again.

She glanced up. Strange. How had she arrived here? At the bottom steps of this place? The springhouse better known as the fairy house. Weird, a stream of mist floated from the arched opening.

Madison climbed the rock stairs up the incline. Still the mellow tones called her. She sat on the level spot by the entrance to the fairy house and looked out over the Vanderheim property.

If coming to the past had made any impact at all, she'd learned a few things. One, she wanted Ben, genuine, faithful Ben, to be her friend.

At the mansion, she'd learned to slow down, to take her time. Hadn't she enjoyed helping with the decorations in the ballroom—not rushing like a racehorse and galloping through the job as fast as her legs would go?

Yes. She'd learned her lessons, but what good did that do? Her life—in this world—would never be the same now. She exhaled a deep sigh. Would she ever find her way home?

As if the wind lifted her fears and tossed them to one side, a great burden rose from her shoulders.

Exhaustion overcame her. She sank down and leaned against the side of the fairy house. The flute played a beautiful tune as her eyes grew heavy.

"There you are." Ben grasped his drone and placed it in the carrying case. Now, where was Maddie? He turned to trace his steps to where he'd last seen her. He stopped a moment and listened. Maybe he could pick up the sound of her footsteps or maybe hear her humming a tune. Then he'd head in that direction.

Nothing.

"Maddie, where are you."

No answer.

He secured the drone case in his grip and continued on. Ten more minutes and he caught his breath. To his right, the terrain rose in an incline about thirty feet. At the top, as if growing out of the mountain, a small building with a rounded roof sat at the top of a series of stairs.

The fairy house? Had he found it?

He took a few leaps up the dilapidated rock steps and squinted.

Someone lay hunched over at the top on a small platform of sorts. Maddie?

He raced up the steps, careful not to trip where several of the stairs had worn away and lay in crumbles.

Puffing, he arrived at the top and the slumbering figure at the side of the house. His heart pounded out of his chest. The fairy house and Maddie lay against it, a small cut on her forehead. Had she been knocked unconscious?

Plink, plink, plink. Drops of water hit the stones near her head. Flutters wafted a breeze to her cheek then she saw a flashing illumination.

The tiny iridescent wings reflected light as the prisms after a rainy day. Three pairs of eyes watched her, one of sapphire, the second emerald and the third a tawny jasper. The wings charged the air with buzzing.

She jumped as a cold drip landed on her nose.

"Maddie, Maddie. Are you okay?" A warm hand

caressed her cheek.

Maddie? Benjamin always called her Madison. He must have come looking for her. "Did you finish watering the other tree?"

"Tree, what tree?"

Maddie opened her eyes.

Ben, his cheeks covered with his usual shadow of whiskers, held her hand. "Oh, Maddie, what happened?"

She sat up and looked around.

Ben's drone case lay on the ground not more than twenty feet from them close to the bottom stairs. He wore his same heavy black jacket and jeans. A ball cap covered his forehead.

A sense of euphoria shot through her like a lightning bolt along with a feeling of peace. The man in front of her was Ben, the drone operator, the kind and gentle man who cared about her.

He stared at her. "Are you hurt?"

She threw her arms around him and drew him closer. "Ben, I'm so very glad to see you. You'll never know how much." She hugged his neck for a few moments and then kissed his cheek.

Ben sat back and stared at her. "Are you all right?"

"Yes, yes." She giggled. She pulled him near again. "If I didn't know better, I'd say I'm in love with you."

"Yeah? After our argument?" Ben settled close to her on the rocks and placed his arm around her shoulders.

"That argument made me realize something." She cuddled closer.

"Yeah, what?"

"I owe you an apology, for everything. For today,

for the way I treated you in the past. I'm sorry."

"I'm not sure what happened to you, but I like this new Maddie," he whispered in her ear. "I've been in love with you since we were kids."

She didn't care what he thought about her now. "Will you hurry up and kiss me?"

"If you promise to explain what's gotten into you."

Chapter Twenty-One

Ben's pulse pounded in his veins as Maddie's lips caressed his. How could he break away from her embrace? But concerns of her welfare sent pangs of alarm through him. He leaned a few inches away and studied her face with the small cut on her forehead. Was the wound serious enough to bring on this change in her? She'd never given him any indication that she cared for him much less wanted to kiss him.

He reached out to touch her forehead with the back of his hand. "You feel cool. No fever, I don't believe."

A grin as wide as the pancakes he'd eaten for breakfast spread across her face. "I did take a fall, right?"

"Yes, apparently right here at the top of the fairy house." He pumped his fist in the air. "The fairy house. You must've come across it while I was looking for my drone."

She rubbed her forehead with an easy touch and then frowned. "How many days did it take you to find your equipment?"

He frowned. "Days? What do you mean? I found it within a half hour and then started to hunt for you."

Maddie groaned. "What is today?"

"Maddie, are you okay? This is Thursday, December nineteenth. You know, we drove up to Travisburg yesterday, had a flat tire, and stayed in the Heidelburg Inn last night." Ben ran a hand through his hair. Should he get her to a doctor?

Maddie stood to her feet, swaying a little.

Ben reached to steady her, and she leaned against him a moment, making his heart race. He glanced at the amazing fairy house they'd searched for. Maddie had discovered it. "I'm getting you into town to see a doctor. That's more important than taking shots of the fairy house. We have to come back tomorrow, anyway."

"Don't be silly. I'm fine except I'll have to admit, I'm a little confused."

"I can tell from the way you're acting. Are you sure you don't want me to take you for help?" If she continued to ask crazy questions, he'd insist she see a doctor whether she liked it or not.

"Help me find my camera before it gets too dark. I want to get some shots of the house lit up for Christmas."

A camera case lay a few feet down the stairs, partly under a bush. He reached for it, praying that her equipment wouldn't be damaged.

Her face lit with joy as he passed the case to her. She opened the bag and glanced inside, lifting the Nikon from its spot and turning it over a couple of times. "It pays to purchase good camera cases. Looks like it survived the fall." She grinned. "Weird."

"What's weird."

"The camera didn't make the journey to … "

"Okay, Maddie. You're scaring me, again. Any

more crazy statements like that and I am taking you into Travisburg to a clinic."

She placed her hand over her mouth. "Sorry." Lifting her camera to snap a picture of the fairy house, she focused and took several shots. "Maybe we can come back tomorrow and get some more pics now that we know where the fairy house is."

As soon as they returned to the mansion, he'd take a few nighttime aerial shots of the house. But after that, he wasn't sure. The strange new Maddie confused him.

Maddie placed her Nikon back in the bag and sauntered down the hill, stepping around the moss-covered and crumbling steps.

Ben stared at her. "Er, Maddie, you seem to know your way around the path and those steps."

"We need to get back to the mansion." Maddie glanced down at her jeans, glad she'd changed from the outfit Ethel had loaned her.

Ethel?

Wait.

Had she dreamed she'd visited the Vanderheim mansion in the 1940's, or had she actually gone there? She pulled the soft blue hood, laundered by Mr. Vanderheim's servant, over her head as she shivered. It had seemed so real. But then if she'd spent several days with Ethel, Robert, and Benjamin, why had only a few hours passed in the present?

She grasped her head and swayed, balancing herself with her other hand on a nearby tree. Thankfully Ben didn't insist she go to the doctor—which was the last thing she wanted to do. She'd have to explain to the personnel at the check-in desk. "Oh, I visited the 1940's for a few days and came back again on the same day." Yep. They'd admit her to a mental institution.

"Okay, but promise you'll tell me if you feel woozy."

"All right." Woozy? She already did, but the more she maneuvered around, the better she felt.

Ben glanced toward the sky. "We'd better get to the mansion then. It's almost dark."

"That's fine. I need some night shots of the exterior. We can do the interior tomorrow." She took the rest of the steps down the hill.

Her mouth turned dry. How could these rocks have been clean and moss-free only what seemed moments ago and now they were deteriorated and covered with years of dirt and debris?

They crossed the bridge over the little creek, the only part of the area which seemed the same, and trekked to the house.

They walked around the leafless trees which still stood in rows of what used to be the well-kept orchard.

Maddie's chest tightened. The garden in front of the house now consisted of knee-high and dead brown grass. Weeds and fallen branches littered the spot where Benjamin's pansies and violas had grown. The flagstones were faded to a dull brown and others lay in fragments.

Beside her, Ben placed his hand on her shoulder. "You look so sad?"

"Oh, I suppose I imagined what the gardens looked like back in Vanderheim's day. I would love to see them restored."

"Perhaps the locals might take it on as a community project." His warm palm lingered on her shoulder.

"I'll ask Ms. Maddox about it." Maddie had never been community-minded before but perhaps that would change. She caught her breath as they neared the mansion. Though the building was the same structure she'd seen only hours ago, the sight of aging shingles and logs on the exterior as well as the brick chimneys smeared with years of dirt and soot sent a shiver down her back.

As they approached the steps to the wide porch, Maddie yelped as the hair on her neck stood up.

Ben leaped toward her. "What is it?"

"Those two Japanese Maples on either side of the road." She pointed to the tree with scarlet and amber bark and grasped her throat.

"Okay." Ben drew out the syllables in one long word. "Is there something about them that bothers you?"

"They've grown at least seventy feet tall, taller than the house."

"From what I understand, a mature Japanese Maple can grow as high as eighty feet."

Maddie squeezed her eyes shut and opened them again. She couldn't let him see her startled reactions any longer. Maybe she'd tell him later, but today wasn't the right time. "You're right of course. I remembered them being smaller."

"No, problem. Let's finish up with the project and get you back to the inn."

In the entry, the grand staircase remained the same. Ms. Maddox approached. "How's your shoot going? I hope you got what you needed."

Ben clenched his jaw. "A few problems." He glanced at Madison. "Overall, well."

No doubt, he referred to the fall at the spring house. He had no idea what occurred after that. "I need a few pictures of the Christmas lights on the outside of the house. But first, may I peek in the room where the Memories of Christmas Ball will be held?" Maddie headed toward the ballroom.

"I see you know the way. Have you been in the mansion before?"

What was Madison to say? *Back in 1940 I helped decorate the hall.* "No, only in pictures."

"All right, then. Take as many photos as you'd like. Anabel's staff has worked hard to get the room ready. They referenced the old photos from the first year the ball was held and tried to recreate the original design."

"I understand how hard Ethel, er I mean you and your staff have worked."

"Who did you mention?"

"Sorry, a slip of the tongue." Maddie took a long breath and held it as she walked toward the ballroom. Placing her hand on the doorknob, she slowly exhaled. Would the magnificent space look the same as when she'd helped Ethel and the servants to prepare the room?

Maddie turned the knob and entered the beautifully decorated area.

Near the stained-glass windows, chairs were set up for musicians. A decorated tree with antique ornaments stood halfway down the side of one wall next to the elegant red velvet chairs. What looked to be the same garland was strung across the ceiling.

Maddie steadied herself with her hand on a nearby chair. She halfway expected to see Ethel in one of her stylish frocks enter the room followed by a couple of servants. Had Maddie returned once again to the Vanderheim's era?

Chapter Twenty-two

Maddie turned over in the comfortable bed in the Vanderheim mansion. Sun streaming in from the window warmed her face. What would the cook prepare for breakfast, and what new ensemble had Ethel laid out for her?

Benjamin. No, she'd rather avoid him if possible.

An odd sound like dancing fairies echoed on the bedside table.

Fairies.

The little creatures that lived and played at the springhouse.

She glanced around. Her phone sat next to her bed. The device must've produced the fairy-sounding jingle.

Oh, yes. The ring tone for when she received a text.

She shook her head to get her thoughts straight which right now seemed askew.

She took a deep breath. Now she knew. She'd returned to her real life. Like she'd shed those extra ten pounds, her insides felt as light as if she'd traveled in a spaceship.

She sat up in bed and glanced out the window. A Tesla Roadster turned a corner on the road below, and a couple of women with shopping bags hooked on their arms strolled down the sidewalk.

She wasn't in the mansion, nor would she have to see Benjamin. Her heart leapt into her chest. She was at the Heidelburg Inn. She and Ben would return to the property once more and then head home.

She grabbed her phone to read the text.

Meet me in thirty minutes for breakfast?

Home. Maddie couldn't think of a better destination.

I can't wait. See you soon.

Ben did a double take between bites of hot oatmeal sprinkled with brown sugar and pecans. From across the table, why was Maddie looking at him like that? "Are you feeling better?"

Maddie leaned closer and smoothed her hand across his cheek. "Hmm. I like this—your prickly whiskers."

When would Maddie get back to her old self? Never, he hoped. "Yeah, it's kind of the style these days instead of shaving it all off."

She nodded. "Yes, I know. It's just … " Her gaze seemed to be fixed on the wall over his shoulder. "I'm sorry. I'm not myself today." She giggled. "I'm better. I'm so happy to be having breakfast with you today."

Ben widened his eyes. "Er, I'm happy to be with you, too." She had no way of knowing how happy he was. He loved this new Maddie. Maybe he finally had a chance with her.

Again, Maddie focused on him, leaning closer, and appeared to inspect every inch of his face. Then she picked up his hand, studied it, and placed it on the table again.

"Okay, now, Maddie. I'm getting worried. You're acting weird. Is there something wrong with me, the way I look?"

Her smile said she'd never felt happier. "Oh, no. Everything is right with you."

"Do you want to tell me what's going on?"

Again, she stared at him, as if he were a different person. "I think I will. Just not today."

Maddie walked up the now familiar stairs of the mansion.

"Where are you going to start?" Ben asked.

"I need some shots of the upstairs."

"Meet you back here in about an hour?"

"Yep. Sounds good. I should be finished by then."

Ms. Maddox approached from a desk near the stairs to the second floor. "Back for one more day?"

"Yes. I'd like to get some shots of the upstairs. Will that be okay?"

"Of course." She pulled an envelope out of her pocket. "We'd also like to invite you to the ball on Christmas Eve. The owner appreciates the hard work you two have done."

Maddie reached for the tickets. "Thank you. I'm sure Ben will be available to come as well."

"The owner has requested that a staff member accompanies anyone who ventures upstairs. I'll go today."

"No problem." Maddie ascended the stairs as she'd done every day when she'd visited before. After several shots of the hall, she paused at the door to the room where Robert and Benjamin had put her that first night. "May I go in here?"

Ms. Maddox tried the door. "Sorry, locked."

Maddie's heart fell into her stomach. She needed to say goodbye to the Vanderheim mansion and the bedroom where she'd spent a lot of time during her visit. She would never want to return, but a nagging sentimental nudge told her she needed this last farewell. Disappointment pestered her, but she shrugged. "All right." She continued down the hall.

"Wait. I have some keys." Fishing in her pocket, Ms. Maddox pulled out a key ring. "Maybe one will fit the door." After going through ten keys, number eleven moved the lock to the right, and the door opened.

Maddie caught her breath. The same bedroom lay before her—the same she'd stayed in only a day ago, yet in reality eighty years in the past.

She strolled to the bed, resting her hand on the pillow where she'd laid her head. The chair she'd sat in when she'd become dizzy remained under the window, and if she didn't know better, the view outside hadn't changed.

"What shots are you planning on taking?" Ms. Maddox's words brought her back to the present.

"Oh, yes. I suppose I was daydreaming for a moment." More like reliving her life in 1940. She lifted her camera, the one she'd worried about, and took shots of the fireplace, the white tiled bathroom with the enameled claw-foot tub, and the small closet.

At the closet, she slowly rotated the door knob. She

peered inside and flinched, clutching her fingers to her chest.

Several dresses hung on a metal bar. She flipped through and paused at the next to last one, a navy wool dress with ruffled sleeves. The dress Ethel had loaned her the first night she slept at the mansion.

Chapter Twenty-three

Waking up in his own bed after spending a few nights in a B and B did Ben good. Something about the familiar, the routine, yet he couldn't deny he'd enjoyed the adventure of the trip to Travisburg.

He stood, stretched, and then did twenty pushups on the rug beside his bed. His bedside clock indicated the date—Saturday, December 21. Only a few more days and they'd head back to Travisburg on Christmas Eve to attend the Memories of Christmas Ball held by the owner, Anabel Thatcher. His pulse picked up speed. A date with Maddie although she might consider it a working date.

His drone work waited in preparation of Monday's meeting with Kendrick Grayson. He needed to upload his images and videos to the computer, edit some of his pictures, and email everything to the boss. A good half day job.

That spirit of adventure tapped him on the shoulder, again. He could do the computer stuff later this afternoon and evening. Instead, he wanted to see Maddie. Maybe take a hike at the Donaldson Gap State Park. Wasn't he one for spontaneity like Maddie said?

He pulled out his cell phone and pressed her speed

dial. "Hey, Maddie. I need to decompress, to do some hiking at Donaldson Gap. Meet me in an hour at the entrance?"

Maddie removed her wool cap and shook her head, allowing her hair to hang around her shoulders. She lifted her face to the sun to enjoy the warmth of the rays. "Good idea you had, Ben. We need a morning in the forest to appreciate this beautiful day. It's not always that we can hike in the winter with the sun shining."

"Yes, and I'd like to debrief about our trip. A lot has changed."

He could say that again, but could she share the events of the last several days with him? Or the strange experience?

As she'd asked herself a thousand times since they'd returned, had she dreamed all that happened or had she actually sat at the Vanderheim table for dinner and met a guy named Benjamin who looked exactly like the man in front of her? Had she really worn clothes popular in the 1940's or chatted with the delightful Ethel who'd fallen in love with Robert? It had all seemed so real.

Ben beckoned her toward the trailhead. "Restoration Trail is a good hike for a winter day. I've taken it a few times. The scenery is spectacular, and the paths are always clear."

"I'm ready." She caught up to walk beside him. After a half mile of steep assent from the valley,

Maddie tightened the laces on her hiking shoes. "You said you needed to talk. What did you want to discuss?" She knew what she wished she could talk about, but would Ben think she'd lost her senses if she told him what she believed she'd experienced?

He rubbed the back of his neck and faced her. "Something happened on that trip, and I'm not sure what. For one thing, you're a different Maddie than the girl I used to know."

They hiked farther and paused on the bridge that spanned a small stream. She propped herself against the sturdy wire and wood railing. "I am different, Ben. Something happened when I found the fairy house." But how much more did she feel comfortable in telling him? If she did explain, would he decide he didn't want to hang out with her anymore? Guys weren't as fanciful as women, she'd always believed. "Did you read fairytales when you were a child?"

"You're scaring me again. Talking crazy like you did after I found you unconscious at the top of those stairs."

"Growing up, I always thought girls read fairy tales and boys read adventure stories. What happened to me at the Vanderheims seemed more like a fairytale. I can't figure out whether I dreamed the events or if the experience actually occurred."

Ben pointed to a couple of tree stumps on the other side of the bridge. "How about we sit down for a while, and you tell me."

"Only if you promise to still be my friend afterward."

"I feel like we're in grade school again." Ben raised three fingers and grinned. "I promise."

Maddie settled on the stump and gazed out over the evergreen-covered valley with patches of snow dotting the landscape. "When you lost your drone, I continued on, trying to find the fairy house. Well, I found it."

"You did." Ben smiled.

"At the top of the springhouse, I slipped and hit my head. I lost consciousness for a moment."

"Yes, I know that. I found you shortly after that."

She put her hand on Ben's. "No. It was six days later."

"Maddie?" He raised his voice."

"I knew you'd react this way."

Ben studied his lap and shook his head. "I'm sorry. Go on."

"You woke me up all right, but you were very, very different. This person said he wanted to be called Benjamin and that he was the gardener and supervisor of the property. He was opinionated and self-centered, looking down on women." She squeezed his hand. "He looked exactly like you but was nothing like you. He made me realize how valuable you, Ben, are to me."

"Thanks, but exactly like me? You mean the way I talk and look and comb my hair?"

"Well, maybe the hair was a little different." She snickered. "But his voice was the same, and he, er didn't stutter. Oh, and he was always clean shaven."

He chuckled. "That's why you were staring at my face the other day."

"Er, yes. Sorry."

"But Maddie, you said you were there six days."

"The owner of the house, Robert Vanderheim, and Benjamin brought me to the mansion."

Ben grasped her arm and turned her to face him.

"Robert Vanderheim was the owner of the mansion. He died years ago." He shook his head.

"I know. Hear me out. His secretary, Ethel, treated me with generosity and kindness." She glanced at a bluebird flitting from one tree to another. "They had a thing for each other, but I don't believe they ever admitted it to each other."

Ben stared at her, a small strand of hair escaping his fuzzy cap. "This is really hard to believe other than … "

"Other than what?"

"You no doubt dreamed this. How could six days pass when I found you within a half hour of leaving you?"

"I don't know, but I remember everything that happened. The preparations for the Memories of Christmas Ball." She tapped his arm. "Ben, I even helped Ethel and the servants put everything in order. When I took my last pictures of the ballroom yesterday, the room was set up exactly like we had decorated it."

"Maybe you'd seen a picture of the ballroom and dreamed about it. And what about your clothes? What did you wear for six days? You had the same clothes on when I came back for you."

"I wore Ethel's outfits the entire time. But I got soaked in the rain and changed into my jeans again before I came back."

Ben shook his head and closed his eyes tight. "It's all too much. How am I to believe that?"

"Oh, I don't know." Maddie swallowed hard. "Even now, I'm not sure if I dreamed what happened or if I traveled backward in time to the year 1940—if that's possible."

Ben held the door for Maddie as she got into his car at the Restoration Trail parking lot. He'd struggled to take in what she'd told him. He knew one thing. She remembered every detail of what she'd thought had happened. He wanted to be her friend—and God willing more, but he'd also needed to keep a close eye on her. If he began to see serious signs of a concussion, once again he'd insist that she see a doctor.

She sat in silence until they had traveled halfway to town. "Ben, you do believe me, right?"

"I believe something happened that day, but neither of us can be sure exactly what. Time will tell."

"Ben, will you go to church with me tomorrow?"

"I'd love nothing better."

She rubbed her hand down his arm. "I'm so glad. The other Benjamin didn't want to have anything to do with church."

Ben gave a small shake of his head. His friend Maddie. She'd think clearer in a few days. "Hey, I have an idea. Why don't we go to the library Monday before our meeting with Kendrick and see if we can come up with any facts about Robert Vanderheim that could help us get to the bottom of this."

"Good idea. Couldn't hurt."

Chapter Twenty-four

Monday morning, Madison parked in the public library lot and glanced around for Ben's car.

Her friend Ben. Always resourceful. And since their meeting with Kendrick wasn't until one, they had time to do some research. If information they found at the library would bring closure on the events at the Vanderheim house, she was all in. At the least, she needed to discover whether she was thinking straight these days.

On the opposite side of the lot, Ben waved and caught up with her. "Good thing the ranger station is closed until the new year. I've got more time to work on our Vanderheim project."

Our project. She liked the sound of that. She hoped her smile told him she was glad to see him.

Inside the library at the information desk, the attendant directed them to the section on Tennessee history. "There are several titles about Robert Vanderheim and his house of fairies." Her eyes sparkled as she spoke the words. "He's quite a legend in our parts."

Madison jotted down the names of the books. "Are you planning to attend the Memories of Christmas Ball tomorrow night?"

"I'd love to, but from what I understand, only selected guests will be there."

Madison winked at Ben. When they arrived at the shelf which held Tennessee history, she laughed. "Does that mean we're selected guests?"

He nodded. "You, especially. It's not everyone who goes unconscious at the fairy house and has a little visit with the Vanderheims."

"It's not everyone who's commissioned to survey the entire property with a drone. That means you're a selected guest, too." She grinned, took a few volumes from the shelf, and grasped his hand, tugging him to the nearby table.

"I can't believe I didn't see these books when I came to research before the trip. I should have asked the librarian." Ben slid in next to her and thumbed through one of the books. "By the way, I remembered to reserve us two rooms at the Heidelburg again."

"Thanks. It'll be nice to dress there instead of wearing our formal attire on the way up." Maddie smiled and then glanced at the contents page of her volume. She ran her finger down the list of chapters and stopped. An aroma reminding her of the pine trees beside the road to the Vanderheim mansion made concentration hard. She leaned toward Ben and sniffed. Yep. His scent made her heart pound faster. Face it. She wanted to remain in his presence, talk to him, smile and laugh with him.

Ben looked her way, and she turned her attention to the table of contents again.

The chapter headings listed the main house, the chicken hatchery, the apple orchard, the horse barn. So far, nothing about his personal life.

Ben nudged her. "Maddie, look at this."

She marked her spot and leaned closer to Ben.

"Read this." He indicated a section on a chapter under the heading: the Vanderheim family.

Maddie slid the book in front of her and lowered her voice. "After completing the massive complex which included a magnificent mansion and gardens, Robert Vanderheim married the woman who served as his secretary for a number of years, an Ethel Hansley. Together they had a daughter, Anabel Vanderheim."

Chills raced up her spine. She wanted to cheer but restrained herself in the quiet library. "Robert and Ethel." She grabbed his arm. "I just knew it. They were so in love."

Ben rolled his eyes and patted her hand. "Maddie, these are people who lived almost a century ago."

He spoke the truth, but she knew them. "And they had a daughter named Anabel. Do you suppose she's the same Anabel selling the mansion?"

Ben grinned. "Read on."

"Their daughter Anabel married a Richard Thatcher. They resided at the Vanderheim mansion until Richard's death."

Maddie stared at the rows of library books, allowing the new information to sink in. Flashes of the mansion's dining room, her bedroom, servants bustling around, the elegant staircase raced through her mind's eye. "So, now we know who Anabel Thatcher is."

"Right. Maybe we can get some more information from her when we attend the ball tomorrow night."

She gripped Ben's hand hard. "I can't believe we'll meet Robert and Ethel's own daughter, their flesh and blood." And perhaps the ball would bring Maddie the closure she needed.

Maddie relaxed in the office chair beside Ben. "I think Kendrick will be pleased with our work." She gave him a smug smile.

Ben nodded and then glanced up as Kendrick walked into the office and took a seat behind his desk. "Sorry, folks. Another matter I had to attend to." He looked at his computer, scrolling through what could've been their files. "Let's see now." He continued to study the screen.

Maddie would've reached for Ben's hand but didn't care to advertise to her boss that she and Ben were on much better terms now than when they left on the trip.

Kendrick looked up. "So, how was Travisburg? Run into any bad weather?"

Ben snickered. "That's an understatement. We got back home safe and sound thanks to the Lord."

Kendrick smiled as he continued perusing the screen. "Ben, your shots are totally amazing. Professional and representative of your outstanding skill. You've provided us exactly what we want. The long shots give an idea of the entire area, and the close shots pick up necessary details."

"Thank you, sir."

If Maddie had looked at Ben's face, no doubt she would've seen his sense of satisfaction.

Kendrick smiled. "I hope you'll be available again soon."

"You can count on that."

He looked up to Maddie. "I had a chance to look at your file earlier, Madison. Your interior pictures portray the beautiful features of the mansion. I can almost imagine what the place would look like when Vanderheim was alive."

Ha, she could imagine exactly how the mansion looked.

"What did you find the most fascinating about the house?"

Maddie sat up straight, eager to talk about her time there. "In the guest bedroom, I loved staring at the pale blue ceiling with the floating clouds. In each of the four corners, I could almost visualize those colorful birds flapping their wings."

Kendrick stared at the screen again and turned it around so she could see it. "I'm not sure where you got that because the ceiling is covered with a tan colored wall paper."

"Oh." She clapped her hand over her mouth. "Well, perhaps I imaged I saw that."

Kendrick laughed. "In any case, hand painted ceilings were common in the days when the home was first built."

Madison swallowed hard. How had she come up with that design, anyway? Had she dreamed it, and why would she tell Kendrick her fanciful thoughts? If only she could come to a resolution about the visit to the Vanderheim mansion.

Kendrick eyed another shot. "This grand staircase is sensational." He squinted and enlarged the shot. "Look at that chaise lounge under the staircase. The wood on the leg toward the back is damaged, as if some creature had chewed on it."

Again, he turned the computer around and tapped on the screen. "See, right there."

Madison threw her head back and laughed. "Oh, that was when Sam was a puppy and chewed some of the wood off. Ethel probably didn't think anyone would notice since the nick was closer to the wall. Besides, she was always so sentimental. She probably couldn't bear to repair what his puppy teeth chewed away."

As soon as the words had left her mouth, Maddie realized she'd misspoken. "I, er, I mean … "

Ben cleared his throat. "Maddie's researched about the Vanderheims. She could have read about this incident in one of the books. Maddie has a great imagination. I think she should become a fiction writer when she's not taking pictures."

Maddie's face burned hot. "Yes, that's right."

"Maddie, you certainly take your work seriously. And I'm most impressed with the photos of the Fairy House. Congratulations on finding it. I hope you get a good rest during the Christmas holidays." Kendrick rested his hand on the receiver on his office phone. "I can't thank you enough. You both did a great job. There is a little bonus in your checks for going the extra mile. Now excuse me, I need to make a call. Merry Christmas."

In the parking lot, Ben drew Maddie toward his car. "I need to show you something. I checked out one of those books we looked at this morning."

Maddie frowned. Now what? She had to admit the past and the present had begun to blur into one landscape, leaving her uncertain which was which. Kendrick was right. She did need a Christmas vacation.

Ben reached into the passenger seat and pulled out a book. He thumbed through a few moments then held the book open to her. "You need to see this. It's the bedroom you spoke of from the year 1940."

Maddie caught her breath and held onto the side of the car.

The shot was of the guest bedroom in which she'd stayed. Though the photo was in black and white, the ceiling was obviously painted with a lighter color to include the clouds and in each corner, birds appeared to flap their wings.

"Maddie, this is the original ceiling in the room. It looks exactly like what you described. You've never been to the estate before, have you?"

She shook her head. "No, never until I went with you."

"Then how did you know what it used to look like underneath the wallpaper? And how did you know they had a dog named Sam? I haven't read anything about him in the references I've looked at? You did, thought, right?"

Maddie lifted her gaze to him and searched his face. "Are you starting to believe me?"

He stepped nearer and wrapped both of his arms around her. She fit perfectly in his embrace, as if she belonged there. For several more moments, she remained next to him. If he could be by her side forever, that was fine with him.

Finally, she leaned away and wiped a tear off her cheek.

"I'm sorry I upset you," he whispered. "Whether you traveled back in time or merely imagined you did, you're here now, and I'm very happy about that. I care for you, Maddie.

Chapter Twenty-five

Madison accepted Ben's hand as he helped her out of his car in front of the mansion. She pulled her white wool coat more snugly around her new emerald-green ballgown as she tried to catch her breath. A tingling sensation fluttered down her back when she glanced at the entrance to the mansion. Icicle lights dangled from the roof's edge outlining the house against the starry night sky. The full moon added its brilliance to the scene. Boughs of pine, tied with red velvet ribbon arched over the carved front door, beckoning them to come in.

Ben passed his keys to the valet and supported her arm as they ascended the stairs to the porch and then walked through the wide entrance.

Warmth infused her entire body, from her arms to her toes. Was it the beautifully decorated entry way she knew so well or the handsome guy in a tuxedo standing beside her? Or maybe both.

Two women in formal gowns stood at the entrance. "Welcome to the Thatcher home and the Memories of Christmas Ball."

The first lady pinned a red rose boutonniere on Ben's lapel. She glanced at Madison. "Allow me to take your coat."

The second woman attached a red rose corsage on Madison's wrist. "And you, my dear, look so lovely in your Christmas green ballgown. The color looks lovely with your red hair."

"Thank you, ma'am." Who didn't like a compliment?

The first lady smiled. "Enjoy your evening."

Madison could get used to the feeling of warmth from Ben's arm around her waist as he guided her into the magnificent room. A string quartet performed under the stained-glass windows in a corner of the room, the same spot Ethel had placed the musicians.

One of the decorated trees against the wall drew her, reminding her of another tree she'd seen recently. "Ben, I wonder how many of these ornaments are new and how many survived the original Vanderheim collection."

The first tree displayed red, green and silver balls with strings of garlands made from fresh cranberries. Madison walked around the side of the tree, and her breath hitched. "Look at this hand-painted silver bulb with poinsettias. I remember this ornament from the day I helped Ethel trim those trees."

Ben gave her a glance that said she was testing his patience. He tugged her closer. "Do you want to go into the dining room? I believe there'll be a section set up with artifacts from the early days of the mansion."

"Oh, yes." Madison allowed Ben to guide her into the area where she'd eaten many meals. "Sorry, but these high heels slow me down a little."

On the opposite end of the room, the hosts had set up a wide table.

Madison's mouth grew dry as she approached. Several scrapbooks lay open. Heavy plastic covered each yellowed page.

A beautiful woman with white hair cut in a short bob, smiled at them. "I want to protect the precious memories of my parents but at the same time would like to share their lives with the citizens of Tennessee."

Madison felt for Ben's hand and squeezed. The woman looked so much like Ethel. The same nose, her eyes. "You're Anabel." She whispered.

Anabel wrinkled her forehead and leaned her head to one side. "Yes, have we met before?"

"No, we haven't." Madison wanted to tell her she'd known her parents before they married but could never say that. "I've read so much about the mansion and your parents that I feel like I know them."

Ben stepped up closer to the table. "We're Maddie and Ben. We work for the real estate company handing your sale. We were here to photograph both the exterior and the interior."

Anabel's eyes sparkled. "I'm glad you came tonight. Take a look at the scrapbooks, and you can get an idea of my life as I grew up here."

Madison looked closer at the first picture in the scrapbook. "The Japanese Maples at the entrance have grown so tall."

"Yes, my father's gardener and property supervisor must've planted those."

Madison's palms turned to ice. "Do—do you have a picture of him in the scrapbook?"

"Yes, one, I believe." She scooted the scrapbook in front of her and turned a few pages. "Here." Anabel put her finger on a small picture.

Heart pounding, Madison glanced at the photo.

A man with the same color of hair as Ben's and about the same build, kneeled on the ground with his back to the camera, placing some kind of flower in the soil.

"Wha, what was his name?"

"Oh, he was Benjamin. He didn't remain in my father's employment long. He left when I was about five."

Madison didn't want to ask what happened to him, but temptation overcame her. "Where did he go?"

Anabel scratched her head. "I believe Mother said he got married and purchased a farm in Georgia."

Madison glanced at the handsome Ben who brought her to the ball. She thanked God that her friend was nothing like Benjamin and that Ben hadn't seen Benjamin's face. She sighed with a deep breath. Who knew how the similarity would've affected him?

Ben laughed. "Benjamin's a good name, I'd say."

For the next twenty minutes, Madison thumbed through the scrapbooks, each page bringing back a memory. A picnic at the outdoor fireplace, Ethel climbing the stairs to the fairy house, Anabel fishing in the creek with her father by her side.

"Oh, Madison." Anabel looked up from her chair. "You might be interested in my mother's diary. Feel free to sit on the couch against the wall—both you and Ben." She passed the small book to Maddie. "But if you don't mind, would you put on these cotton gloves as you handle the book?"

"Of course."

Ben pulled on his gloves and accepted the book she handed him.

Anabel looked at Ben. "That one contains original drawings of my father's design for the mansion, many of the other buildings, and his water features."

"Thanks." Ben slid down beside Madison.

Madison turned to the first page which was dated January of 1940. Ethel began her entry by describing her new job with the wealthy Robert Vanderheim. Maddie skipped some of the days until December of 1940. Ethel talked about as his secretary taking letters for Mr. Vanderheim and preparing for the Memories of Christmas Ball.

Madison paused on December 19th and gawked at the words. *Today, a strange young woman arrived on the property. Benjamin found her unconscious next to the springhouse. Robert called Dr. Dankworth to care for her. Poor creature, she was dirty and wearing men's clothes. I loaned her some of my things.*

Heart pounding out of her chest, Madison turned a page and read the next entry. *Our dear visitor is feeling a bit better today, but I'm still mystified by her. She makes such bizarre statements. And her impertinent comments about my clothes!*

Madison clapped her hand over her mouth and couldn't restrain the smile. If she could talk to Ethel today, would she forgive her for insulting her dresses after the generous woman clothed her for the six days she remained at the mansion?

Madison read a few more entries. *Madison went to church with us today. I've grown to love her as a friend. She encouraged me to open up to a relationship with Robert, which is not at all distasteful to me.*

The next one stopped Madison. *I don't know how to describe the event that occurred today. Madison took a walk in the evening. I get cold chills every time I think of what happened. We never saw her again even though Benjamin searched for her. I have no idea where she went, but I can only pray that she is okay and found her way back to wherever she came from.*

Madison gripped Ben's hand. "You have to read this. This is proof. It means I was here in Robert and Ethel's time."

Ben held the diary in front of him as he read.

If Ben wasn't beside her, she wasn't sure what she would've done. She needed him now, for support, to find sanity again.

Finally, Ben glanced up at her and shook his head. "Maddie, I don't know what to say. Ethel even states your name, Madison."

Madison took a long breath and hung onto Ben's hand beside her on the couch. "The day before I returned home, I went to church with Ethel and Robert. I prayed and thanked God that He transcends time. He's the same then as He is today and will always be."

Ben tapped his finger on an entry a few days after the one she'd read. "Look at this."

Madison accepted the offered diary and read the page he indicated. *We enjoyed the Memories of Christmas Ball this year, and true to what Madison had said, Robert indicated his love for me. Before the ball, he asked me to marry him and gave me my beautiful diamond ring. That same night, one of the ladies in our church congregation asked where Madison was. I told her she'd disappeared. The lady went on to say that she saw Madison out in the graveyard by the church, the day she disappeared. I suppose I'll never know what happened to the dear woman.*

Anabel called from her perch behind the table set up with the artifacts. "So far, what caught your interest in Mother's diary?"

Madison smiled. "I suppose your dad proposing to your mom. It was so romantic. I always knew—" She almost said she'd always believed they were meant for each other and had told her mother so.

"I'm not sure if Mom put this in the diary or not. But she used to tell me the story about something that happened when they first fell in love."

Madison sat up straight on the couch. "I'd love to hear about it."

Anabel's eyes twinkled again with the memories. "Well, it seems Mom had planned a bar-be-que on the patio. Her dress caught on fire by a rogue spark emitted by the fire pit. Dad put it out for her. She always told me that was the spark they needed to fall in love."

Madison's smile had to be as wide as the full moon tonight. She walked toward the table and replaced the diary. "I can't thank you enough for sharing your home and memories with us."

"It will be hard to move, but I want others to enjoy the location my father worked to establish."

After enjoying the hors d'oeuvres and the dancing, Madison touched Ben's shoulder. "One more thing I'd love to do tonight—visit the fairy house."

Ben helped Maddie slip into her coat. "You think you can hike over there in those things?" He nodded toward her heels. Why women wore those shoes on stilts, he'd never understand.

"I have some tennis shoes I left in your car. I can put them on."

If Ben had questioned Maddie before, he no longer did. But though he'd seen proof of what she'd claimed, he couldn't imagine how she went back in time. Other than … Time travel only happened in fantasy books. He shrugged.

He gripped Maddie's hand hard and focused the light from the flashlight that he always left in his car. It illuminated the path. "Be careful. We don't want a repeat of last time."

The shimmery green dress she wore to the ball fit tightly on her attractive curves, which he didn't complain about. Until tonight, he hadn't realized how much her feminine shape enticed him. But taking wide steps didn't work now. Finally, they arrived at the level spot in front of the springhouse.

Ben had never seen Maddie so quiet. She stood motionless peering in the direction of the arch-shaped entrance, no longer covered by a door.

She sighed and slid her arm around his waist. "Do you suppose anyone actually sees fairies, or is it a tale people love to tell? I believe I've seen them, but perhaps the images sprang from my imagination."

"As we know, fireflies or the fairies as people call them hibernate in the winter, so it's doubtful." Ben took a few steps closer to the door to the spring. "But here's an idea. Let's check out the temperature of the spring water."

"Why"?

"You'll see." Ben stepped inside of the house, removed his glove, and stuck his hand in the bubbling water. He caught his breath. Warm water spurted up from the ground. He turned around and almost bumped into Maddie behind him. "Put your hand into the water."

After dipping her fingers into the gurgling flow, she grinned. "Warm enough to take a bath in."

Ben wrapped his arm around her shoulders and savored the moment. Standing in a warm springhouse in the middle of winter with Maddie by his side—what more could he want? He closed his eyes.

"Ben, look." Maddie's voice held surprise, what he could only describe as awe.

Surrounding them, flashing lights darted around, flitting to one side and spinning to the other. Twirling to the ceiling and sailing around the perimeter of the small room, the fireflies seemed to delight in their dance.

Maddie squeezed his hand and snuggled into his arms. "Ben, this is it. We're seeing the fairies on this special occasion—in celebration of Ethel and Robert's life and the Memories of Christmas Ball."

For far too long, Ben had wanted to place his lips on Maddie's, showing her how he felt about her. He swung her around to face him and touched her cheek. "Maddie, I'm going to kiss you if you don't stop me."

Maddie looked at him with her periwinkle eyes that told him she didn't plan to.

Their kiss blessed him as he knew Maddie was the woman the Lord had given him. He held her in his embrace.

Finally, they leaned away from each other. "Merry Christmas, Maddie. I love you."

"It took my trip to the Vanderheim estate to

understand how much I love you. Merry Christmas."

Chapter Twenty-six

Ben's teeth chattered. Was it the cold spring morning or his nerves? He frowned. "Are you sure you have everything? You got the permit? You have the silver box and is the drone battery charged?"

Andy punched his shoulder. "Don't worry, dude. Everything will be okay." He gave him a reassuring grin. "I'll look for you and Maddie at the waterfall around noon but will stay out of sight. I have my binoculars."

"Okay." Ben took a deep breath and scrubbed his chin. "When I give the signal, you send over the drone."

"Wait, what was the signal?" Andy snickered. "Just joking. You'll take off your hat, and then I launch the drone."

"Right." Ben paced a few steps onto the trailhead and out again. "I owe you one, pulling those strings to get the drone permit. You must've impressed your boss when you explained the special occasion. And now you have to go to work in exchange. I hope you find that illegal campsite."

"I will. See you at the falls." Andy gripped the handle of the drone case. "You've got this."

Madison had to speed walk to catch up with Ben's brisk strides. "You must be in a hurry for that picnic lunch."

"Sorry, I'm just excited, er, looking forward to seeing the waterfall."

Maddie exhaled, breathing in the fresh, scented air. So much had changed since their last trek up to Rainbow Falls. Spring had announced its arrival with its glorious wildflowers covering every inch of the landscape.

She stopped and focused her camera for a closeup of the blooms on a plant to the side of the trail. "What are those called?" She nodded to the white flowers that covered the small hills and path edges.

Ben slowed. "Those are white Trillium. Colonies of them bloom in the spring. See those pink ones?" Ben pointed to a few nestled under a mossy rock. "They're the same flower. They turn pink as they age."

Since their job at the Vanderheim estate and her adventure, she'd enjoyed each spare moment with Ben. Getting to know him, his hopes and dreams, his deep thoughts and silly humor—she could listen to him for hours. Those beautiful flowers dotting the landscape announced her joy to all the countryside—and her love for Ben.

Maddie sneaked a peek at the gorgeous guy beside her as he shared some of his ranger knowledge, and her heart sped up.

Now Ben walked so fast she had to jog. "Hey, slow

down." Was he nervous about something? After five minutes, she glanced up and then caught her breath. "Look, the falls."

Ben smiled. "Since the last time we were here, the water has begun to flow because of the spring rains."

She grabbed his arm. "Look, Ben. The prisms." She spread out her red checkered blanket on a wide flat rock. Easing down, she stared at the colorful rainbows shining in the mist of the fall.

Ben edged down next to her and stared at his watch.

"What, are we on a schedule?"

Ben's face turned as pink as the Trillium flowers. "No, no. I guess I'm in the habit of checking the time because of my job." He stood and then sat down again.

"Relax, Ben." She'd never seen him so nervous. "You want a sandwich?"

"No, not right now." He glanced up and gazed toward the trees and then back to her. "There's something I want to talk about."

"Ok." Could the topic be what she thought, what she hoped he'd say?

Ben, stood, taking off his hat. He reached for her hands, lifting her up. "I've loved you since we were teenagers." His breath seemed to catch in his throat. "Not only are you the love of my life, you're my best friend."

A flashing silver caught her eye, and she sucked in a breath. "What is that?" She pointed to a giant dragonfly-like creature heading towards them. "Is that a drone?"

Ben chuckled. "Wait a minute."

The drone slowed and hovered in front of them. A wicker basket, swaying in the wind, hung from cables underneath the machine.

Ben reached for the basket and handed the little container to her. He turned to his left, waved, and the drone sped off.

"What in the world?" Maddie held the basket in front of her like a shy child on Easter.

"Look inside."

She removed a silver box, embossed with small birds. The edges were scrolled with vines and tiny flowers. She turned to face Ben and then gasped, clasping her hand to her throat.

He knelt before her. "Maddie, will you stay with me always and be my wife?"

The birds silenced their noisy song. The breeze stilled. The waterfall quieted. Was all of nature waiting for her answer? Ben's proposal was a once in a lifetime event. *What should I say? I can't imagine life without him.* "Yes! I'll marry you."

Ben rose from his knees and shouted. "She said yes. She said yes." He gathered Maddie into his arms. Leaning back, he stared into her face, as if to remember the moment forever. He lifted her chin with his finger and drew her near, placing his lips on hers.

The silent birds returned to their singing as if offering congratulations.

"Open the box, Maddie."

With trembling fingers, she removed the silver top. A beautiful marque-cut diamond lay on a red velvet pillow inside the box.

"Oh, Ben, it's the most beautiful ring I've ever seen."

"It's for the most beautiful woman I've ever known. I love you."

181

Chapter Twenty-seven

Ben rested his hand on his wife's back, escorting her out the front doors of Parkhill Christian Church. They rushed down the sidewalk toward the limo waiting on the street to take them to the reception and then on to the airport. To think, a honeymoon at Yosemite National Park—one of the most challenging rock-climbing areas of the United States. The lodge within the interior of the park where they had reservations was beautiful, he'd heard.

"Hey, you two." His brother Dave stood at the edge of the sidewalk next to his wife and two kids, along with the other attendees, prepared to deposit a barrage of flower pedals onto Ben and Maddie's heads. Dave gave a thumbs up. "I told you so. Marriage is gonna agree with you."

Ben didn't miss the message his brother and his family communicated. He'd never seen his brother happier. He and his wife were a team—there for each other while raising great kids.

Not even Dave's ribbing bothered him today. Ben waved at them and sneaked a kiss on Maddie's cheek.

Back in high school, he never would've guessed that he'd marry the girl who'd captured his heart.

Maddie, the girl whose friends had teased him relentlessly and turned him into a stuttering mess. How could he have ever known? She loved him as well and wanted to spend her whole life with him.

Inside the elegant limo, he drew the gorgeous woman to his chest and kissed her. "I love you, Maddie Taylor."

Maddie held her husband's hand as they walked out of Parkhill Christian Church and down the stairs. A crowd lined either side of the sidewalk, tossing fresh flower petals on their heads. Like fairies, the pedals floated around and then flittered to the ground.

She lifted the white satin, floor-length fabric as she walked at a brisk pace. The top with the bold lace pattern fit tightly, taking her breath away. Or was it the words, I do, she'd spoken only moments ago to the love her life, Ben Taylor?

Ben helped her into the limousine and rushed around to the other side. After he settled in beside her, Maddie kissed his jaw covered with light brown stubble. His scent, a hint of lavender and sage, propelled her heart into a fast sprint.

Her bouquet of select wildflowers slipped from her hand as Ben turned to her, cuddling her closer to his chest. "I love you, Ben." Barely able to breathe, she clung to him as he laid his lips on hers.

"This is the best day of my life. To think, you agreed to be my wife. In high school, I never would've imagined this day would come."

"Me, either. Hey, have you noticed that your stutter is gone?"

"I guess you don't make me nervous anymore." Ben gently stroked her hand.

"When I first went to the Vanderheim mansion, I never would've predicted what happened. The Benjamin I met who looked exactly like you helped me see the truth. Though he was as handsome as you, there were no other similarities." She laid a kiss on the tip of Ben's nose. "I learned that what's inside a person matters much more than what's outside. He was selfish and chauvinistic. You're considerate and kind." She giggled. "The fairies transported me to another time period where I could discover how precious you are to me in this time period."

"So, you believe that you actually traveled back in time to 1940?" He peered at her.

"Yes, I'm sure." Maddie slipped her arms around her husband once more. "But no fairy could ever take me away from you now."

Epilogue

1 year later

Madison gazed at her gorgeous husband lying on his side with eyes closed. His soft breathing told her he still slept. She slid on her house shoes and padded into their kitchen. She toasted a piece of sourdough bread, poured a cup of decaf coffee, splashed cream on top, and moseyed onto the red cedar deck. The rocking chair she'd painted turquoise invited her to slip down and breathe in the exquisite countryside.

The view of Travisburg always took her breath away. The contrasting hues of the mountains. The dark blues, farther in the distance, contrasted with the lighter greens of the summer foliage closer to their condo—she could never get enough of the beauty.

Fighting a twinge of nausea, she nibbled the toast. Moving to Travisburg hadn't been a burden at all. She and Ben still saw their families in Fairville frequently. Since Ben got his new job with the National Park Service in the White Oak National Park, the location was so much more convenient.

Ben.

She'd never regret marrying him. And now she was

even more proud of him than ever. He'd finally stepped into his dream job. Head landscape architect for White Oak. Each night he came home describing his plans and designs to support the preservation, rehabilitation, and stewardship of their national park, and her heart swelled with pride. Her husband shouldered a great deal of responsibility—and most of all, he loved his work.

A kiss on the back of her neck told her that Ben joined her on the deck. "Good morning, Maddie." Ben slipped into the chair next to her and inhaled a long breath. "Love the mountain air."

She rested her coffee cup on the side table and drew her legs up on the chair's seat. "How did you sleep?"

"Couldn't have asked for a better night's slumber—especially with my wife by my side." He fiddled with the gold band on his left hand.

Should she tell him now what she suspected or wait? "And I slept all night with a forest ranger." She giggled. "I'm so proud of you. Finally using your landscape architecture degree." She blew him a kiss.

"So, what are you up to today?"

"I'm finishing up my book. I'll look for a publisher soon."

"Honey, you've put in so much work. The extensive pictorial representations of the people of Tennessee, past and present. I'm sure you'll have some takers soon."

A bald eagle caught an air current and glided across the clear blue sky. Another followed as soon as the first one landed in a sturdy, leafy tree.

Ben propped his feet on the railing around the deck. "I talked to Andy last week. He's still at Donaldson Trail State Park. He told me a bit of news."

"Oh, yeah?"

"You'll like this. He plans to propose to Melody this weekend."

"Yahoo." Madison clapped her hands. "I know she'll say yes. She is head over heels for him."

"Andy wanted us to go rock climbing with them pretty soon."

Okay. The time had come. "I don't really feel like it right now."

Ben frowned and turned in his chair toward her. "Why? Is something wrong?"

Madison smiled as if she knew a secret. "I'm tired, and to tell you the truth, I can't keep anything down."

Ben stood and drew her to her feet. "You need to get to a doctor. I'm concerned."

She threw her arms around his neck. "I will in the next week or so. But I think I have an accurate diagnosis."

Ben rubbed his chin. "You do?"

She leaned closer and whispered in his ear. "How do you feel about being a daddy in about seven months."

He stared at her a few moments as if she'd spoken in French or German. "You mean … "

"I'm pretty sure I'm going to have a baby."

"I think I like the idea." Ben twirled her around and then set her down. "I'm sorry. I hope I didn't hurt you."

"No, silly. Our baby is only the size of a raspberry right now."

Ben rubbed his eye with his fist and turned his back to her.

If she didn't know better, she'd think her sweet guy had shed a tear.

He turned to her once again. "You'll make an excellent mother."

"Thanks, honey. And when our baby is old enough, I'll read him or her a fairy tale before bedtime. Maybe *The Fairy Garden.* What do you think?"

Ben kissed her cheek. "As long as our child doesn't take the stories too seriously."

The End

About the Authors

June Foster is an award-winning author who began her writing career in an RV roaming around the USA with her husband, Joe. She brags about visiting a location before it becomes the setting in her next contemporary romance or romantic suspense. June's characters find themselves in precarious circumstances where only God can offer redemption and ultimately freedom. To date June has seen publication of over 35 novels and several devotionals.

A reader says of her debut novel Flawless: June Foster is a unique author. She has a way of looking at people and seeing what's on the inside and not what's on the outside. She loves to bring characters with unique personalities and problems to the written page.

Find June Foster at junefoster.com.

Kelly Cordova lives in Texas with her husband, Tom, where she homeschooled their six children. Before settling in El Paso, she and her husband served as missionaries in Peru. Kelly has a bachelor's degree in photojournalism and a Master's in public affairs journalism. *Eliza's Hope* is Kelly's debut novel.

If you enjoyed The Other Side of the Fairy House, check out some of June's other titles.
The Woodlyn Series
Flawless
Out of Control
All Things New

The Almond Tree Series
For All Eternity
Echoes From the Past
What God Knew
Almond Street Mission

Small Town Romance Series
Letting Go
Prescription for Romance
A Harvest of Blessings
The Long Way Home

The Cranberry Cove Series
The Inn at Cranberry Cove
Love Found at Cranberry Cove
Christmas at Cranberry Cove
A Home in Cranberry Cove
Danger in Cranberry Cove

The Ford Family Ranch Series
The Novice Ranch Hand

Christmas Novellas
Christmas at Raccoon Creek

A Christmas Kiss
A Kiss Under the Mistletoe

Devotional
Dancing in a Field of Daisies

Short Stories
Someone to Call His Own
An Accidental Kiss

Stand Alone Titles
Red and the Wolf
Misty Hollow
Lavender Fields Inn
Restoration of the Heart
A Home for Fritz
Dreams Deferred
An Unexpected Family
Ryan's Father
Eliza's Hope

About the bestselling Cranberry Cove series.

***The Inn at Cranberry Cove* – first place 2021 Selah winner in romantic suspense— Blue Ridge Mountain Christian Conference**
Ashton Price arrives in Cranberry Cove, Washington, her pride wounded by her former boss.

James Atwood endures punishing guilt after the death of his wife and son. Together, they must discover the mystery that haunts the Inn at Cranberry Cove. **The Inn at Cranberry Cove**

Book two continues the story: *Love Found at Cranberry Cove*

Gracie Mayberry wants to study marine science at the community college in a neighboring coastal town. Seattle resident Blake Sloan admits he's followed his father's dream instead of his heart's desire—to run his own business and start a non-profit to benefit wounded vets. But when a stalker makes terrifying midnight visits to the humble Mayberry home and threatens their lives, Blake discovers he's also a target of extortion. Can Blake and Gracie learn who's behind the danger that threatens them? Will a small-town girl and big-city boy find a life together? **Love Found at Cranberry Cove**

In Book three: *Christmas at Cranberry Cove*

Ryder Langston retires from commercial fishing and manages Blake Sloan's supply stores. When the owner of the inn in Cranberry Cove hires a new executive chef, Ryder is intrigued by the tall woman with ebony hair who hides a dark family secret.

Juliette Duplay must flee from her French roots and her past when a family member turns against her. She'd like to blend into the American culture but can't escape danger even in the small community of Cranberry Cove.

Can Ryder and Juliette unravel the mystery in time

to celebrate *Christmas at Cranberry Cove?* **Christmas at Cranberry Cove**

In Book four, Madison and Micah run from their past. *A Home in Cranberry Cove*

Madison Mitchell will never trust a man again. The love of her life broke her heart and married a French chef. Now she throws herself into her work at The Inn at Cranberry Cove. When she accidentally tangles with the manager of a nearby fishing supply store, she suspects the handsome guy is hiding something.

Micah Collins flees Sacramento seeking solace in the seaside village in Washington state. But he discovers an enemy has followed him to Cranberry Cove. He must endure frightful threats at the same time keeping his previous life secret. When Madison finds herself in danger, Micah blames himself.

Madison and Micah are haunted by someone from Micah's past, but is the culprit the real enemy or should they look elsewhere? Will they find a future together? **A Home in Cranberry Cove**

Book Five *Danger in Cranberry Cove* **Julie and Lucas discover a 15-year-old secret.**

When Julie Wilder joins local lawyer Lucas Ethridge in uncovering clues of who murdered their high school friend on the beach fifteen years before, anonymous phone calls from someone who claims to be the killer are unnerving. After incriminating evidence turns up, can Lucas and Julie discover the killer's

identity or will they suffer the same fate as their friend?
Danger in Cranberry Cove